C000101655

BEAR AND

SHADOW OF WHITE
BOOK 2

Blake J Soder

MAY 3

Dean set his leather punch and mallet down on the table in front of himself, taking a break from the belt he was working on. He made fists with both hands, slowly opening and closing them, stretching and flexing his fingers to work the stiffness out. This damn cold was playing hell with his arthritis.

There was an old calendar on the wall above his cluttered worktable, its pages yellowed and curled at the edges. On the top half was a faded picture of a leggy, blue-eyed blonde in a red bikini sprawled seductively across the hood of some fancy yellow sports car. The calendar part below the picture said it was the third day of May. The year had been crossed out and rewritten twenty times. He'd heard once that calendars tended to repeat every so many years. So, while it might not really be the first week of May, Dean figured it was at least in the ballpark. Hell, there was even a chance that today really was May the third.

He looked to the window of his shop. The snow that had begun this morning was still coming down hard and steady. There was already a good four inches of new snow on top of the twelve from yesterday. By the time it was over, there would probably be two feet or more. Twenty years ago, before the world went to hell and the weather followed, this would have been considered late spring. Not anymore. Spring had been arriving later and later every year. Summers were ever-shorter and winters weren't even giving autumn a chance. Soon, Dean figured, he'd oversleep one morning and find he'd missed spring and summer entirely.

He flexed his fingers a few more times and then eased off his work stool. Every joint in his body protested the movement with dull, aching pain. He put his hands on his hips and stretched his back, letting out a groan. Turning, he made his way through the clutter of tables, tools, and racks to the woodstove in the center of his small shop.

He had long ago cleaned out the tools of his old trade, back when he was a skilled, young carpenter making over-priced, custom cabinets and furniture for the trendy well-to-do. At sixty-three, he was twenty years older now and there just wasn't much call for hand-made furniture anymore – not any call for it, actually. Instead of woodworking tools, his shop was now filled with farming tools needing repair, knives, axes, and saws waiting to be sharpened, and various wooden racks with animal hides stretched out on them, ready to be turned into coats, gloves, boots, or whatever else someone might need. Baskets of smoked meats and dried fruits and vegetables hung from the ceiling.

He poked a few more pieces of wood into the stove and stood next to it for a while, letting the warmth work its way into his muscles and joints. It wasn't even noon yet but he was debating taking the rest of the day off. Maybe go home and sit in front of his fireplace, drink a little wine, take a nap. Hell, who was going to complain?

As he was turning to warm his backside, three slow, heavy thuds shook the front door to his shop.

"Come on in, Bear," Dean hollered, hoping to stop the man before he added a few more dents to the outside of his door with that big goddamn stick of his. The bear came around only three or four times a year, but no one else knocked on his door like that, if they even bothered to knock at all.

The door opened and the bear stepped in, filling the doorway. A bit over six feet tall with broad shoulders, he had long brown hair and a thick, untrimmed beard that hid most of his face. His hard, hazel eyes and the weathered creases of his forehead gave him the look of a man much older than Dean knew he was.

The bear got his name from the long, bear-hide coat he wore. Dean knew it weighed more than fifty pounds. He had tanned and trimmed it himself nearly eighteen years ago. The bear almost always wore the coat open, even in weather like this. Beneath the coat, he wore a hand-stitched, deerskin jerkin, pants, and leather boots, also products of Dean's leather-working skills.

The bear gave Dean a slight nod in greeting as he closed the door, snow falling from his hair and shoulders onto the floor.

"One of these days," Dean said, "you're going to crack my door right down the middle, banging on it with that goddamned stick." He made his way back to the shelves next to his workbench. "You could knock like a human being, you know, instead of thumping like some half-ignorant cave man."

The bear grunted and leaned his staff against the wall. It was a seven-foot piece of hickory almost three inches thick. Dean had a feeling the bear used it for more than just walking and banging on his door. Something that big and heavy could be a formidable weapon in the hands of a man big enough to swing it, someone about the size of the bear.

A canvas duffel bag was slung over the bear's shoulder. He set the bag on the heavy wooden table just inside the door of the shop and then shrugged out of his coat. He shook the snow off and then hung it on a thick wooden peg on the wall by the door. Dean had installed the peg a few years ago to accommodate the bear's heavy coat.

"Figured you'd be here sooner," Dean called over his shoulder. "Got to thinkin' maybe you'd finally met something tougher than yourself and you were layin' dead in the woods somewhere."

"Not this year," the bear said. He took a seat at the table and watched as Dean plucked a pair of boots off the shelf.

"Had these ready a month ago," Dean said, turning and crossing the cluttered floor again. When he reached the table, he thumped the boots down next to the bear's duffel bag. He lowered himself into a chair on the opposite side and took a minute to catch his breath.

"You doing okay?" the bear asked, eyeing him with concern. "You seem a little winded."

Dean brushed it off. "Just a little stiff is all. Me and cold weather don't get along as well as we used to." He nodded to the boots on the table between them. "You going to give those a try or are you just going to take my word for it they fit you?"

The bear eyed him a little longer and then bent down and began unlacing his old boots.

Dean had been trading with the bear for almost eighteen years now. The big, intimidating man sitting across from him had been little more than a gangly kid when he'd first showed up at his door, wearing worn-out boots and layers of thread-bare clothes. He hadn't even been old enough to grow a passable beard. But the still-bloody hide of a grizzly bear slung over his shoulder was proof enough the kid was already tougher than hell. Unconcerned he was in danger of bleeding to death from the horrendous wounds the grizzly had inflicted on him, he'd asked Dean if he could make a coat for him from the bear's hide.

Dean had taken the kid in, stitched his wounds, and agreed to make the coat if he would stay a week or two until he was healed enough to return to wherever the hell he came from. Only later, while preparing the hide, did Dean notice the animal did not die from a bullet, an arrow, or even a sharp stick, but from a single, savage knife wound to the side of its neck. The placement and angle of the wound indicated the bear had been on top of the kid when the wound was inflicted.

He remembered asking the kid his name all those years ago but it no longer mattered what his answer had been. As far as Dean was concerned, anyone who could take on a full-grown grizzly bear with just a knife and come out on top deserved not only the bear's hide but also its name.

Four or five times a year, usually in early spring and late fall, the bear would return to his shop, always with skins, often with other items of trade. When people in the village or random travelers asked Dean about him, he could tell them only that the bear came from the woods and the bear returned to the woods. Dean figured he traveled north in the summer and south for the winter, following the animals he hunted. Outside of that, Dean knew little else about him.

The bear removed his old boots and laced the new ones on. He stood and walked a few steps across the room and then back again. He nodded appreciatively.

"These are good."

"God damn right they're good. That's top-grade cowhide lined with beaver pelt. The bottom of the soles is steel-belted tire rubber, glued and double-stitched to leather with extra heavy lacing. If you wear this pair out any sooner than next year, I'll eat what's left."

"I'm going to remember you said that," the bear replied, grinning beneath his beard. "I'm heading up to the Dakotas soon – mighty rough country up there. Next time I see you, I may be handing you a fork and knife."

He opened the duffel bag and pulled out two deer hides and a fistful of rabbit skins. He laid them on the table.

"What's this?" Dean picked up one of the deer hides and examined it. "You wanting me to make you something else? You already traded me for the boots."

The bear shook his head. "They're for you, straight up. No trade."

"And here I didn't get you nothin' but the best goddamn pair of boots ever made." He ran his palm across the smooth side of the deer hide. "I'll consider these a tip. Did you scrape and work these like I showed you?"

"As best I could," the bear said, sitting back down. "Might be a little rough. Only so much I can do in the woods."

"I see that. You still suck at it but at least you're getting better." He pushed the hides aside. "You got time for a drink? Took a couple bottles of wine in trade the other day. Blackberry, I think. Or are you on your way to slaughter more helpless little animals so you can eat their flesh and wear their skins?"

"It's the natural order of things."

"Yeah, yeah. Kill or be killed. Eat or be eaten. Justify your murderous rampage against nature any way you want. You got time for that drink or not?"

"Got something better for you." The bear once again reached into his duffel bag and this time pulled out two large, brown clay jugs with hinged, swing-top caps. He slid one across the table to Dean.

"What the hell is this?" Dean looked the jug over as though it might be booby-trapped. "You find some old swamp water with just enough dysentery in it to give it a kick?"

"It's beer, you cantankerous old bastard. A guy I know down south brews a batch every now and again."

"Beer? No shit?" He pushed the wire hinge up with his thumbs, flipping the cap over. A satisfying hiss escaped. "Ah, by the gods! Never thought I'd hear that sound again." He leaned forward, closed his eyes, and inhaled the aroma.

"You mentioned last time how much you missed a cold beer."

"What'd you have to give for these? Your soul?"

"He doesn't really trade in souls but I got him to part with these for a couple pounds of sugar and five pounds of jerky."

"Jesus, he got a deal!"

The bear gave a slight shrug. "All depends on what you want and what you've got to trade."

Dean hefted the growler in a toast.

"To you, my Neanderthal friend. May you always run faster than whatever's trying to eat you."

The bear nodded to him and returned the toast.

"And may you one day get that corncob out of your ass, you crusty old fart."

They each took a long drink.

Dean closed his eyes, savoring the flavor. "Now *that's* beer."

"If you say so. Never really drank much beer before."

"Didn't drink beer? What the hell else is there but wine and beer?"

"Brandy, whiskey, vodka, mead…"

"Brandy? Vodka? Shit. Fancy drinks for fancy people. And what the hell is mead?" Dean cocked his head at the bear. "You got some hidden past I don't know about?"

The bear hesitated and then raised his growler again. "I gave up my past a long time ago," he said before taking another drink.

The bear never talked about where he came from and he didn't like people asking. Dean took another drink himself and changed the subject.

"You seen any signs of spring yet?"

"It's coming. Ice on the river's starting to break up. Give it another two, three weeks."

"Gettin' later every year."

"Yeah, you might want to start thinking of packing up and heading south. A lot of people have."

"What about you?"

The bear made a noncommittal shrug. "I follow the animals. I go where they go."

"That reminds me," Dean said. "Had a couple guys pass through here last week. Came down from Canada, heading for Kansas or Colorado. They said it's already permanent snowpack up there in the north, even in the summer. You heard anything about that?"

The bear nodded. "I was up a ways into Canada last summer. Must have been August or September. Still had snow on the ground and ice on the smaller lakes."

"Ah, it's fucking Canada anyway," Dean said and took another drink. "Full of goddamn moose and Frenchmen. Who gives a shit?"

"Maybe you will in a few years if this cycle doesn't break soon." The bear took another pull of beer and leaned back in his chair, glancing around the shop. "Do any trading with them?"

"Who? The Canadians? Fixed 'em up with some of your smoked venison and fish in exchange for an old rifle with a busted firing pin."

"What the hell kind of trade was that?"

"Look who's asking. Two pounds of sugar and five pounds of meat for two beers?" Dean shook his head. "Anyway, Roland's been hanging around here a lot. You know him. Big guy. Keeps hogs out by the lake. He's pretty good with his hands so I figure maybe I can set him up with a workbench here and he can do a little firearms repair every now and again."

"Had much of a call for that?"

"Some, but my hands aren't steady enough for that kind of work anymore. Be good to have an apprentice to help out once in a while. Could maybe even teach him some leather work."

The sound of the door opening caused them both to turn and look. A thin, young man in his late twenties with a few wisps of beard on his chin stepped in, stomping the snow from his boots. He was wearing a camouflage army jacket over a hooded sweatshirt.

"Don't bother knocking there," Dean growled at him. "Good way to get your dumb ass blown off these days."

"Huh?" The young man looked up at him and then glanced quickly around the shop. "I was told this is where I can do some trading. Thought you were open."

"I do the tradin' and you do the knockin', shit for brains."

The man mumbled an apology and closed the door behind himself. He stuffed his hands into his jacket pockets and hunched his shoulders forward as he stomped the snow from his boots. Glancing up again, he caught sight of the growlers on the table. His eyes went a little wider.

"Is that beer?"

"It's moose piss and coal tar," Dean said, still not cutting the kid any slack. "Good stuff if you can get it. Now what the hell are you looking for and what do you have to trade?"

"Oh... um... I was wondering if... if you had a rifle. You know... for hunting." The kid was glancing around the shop again.

Dean looked over at the bear. The bear said nothing, his face expressionless, his eyes fixed on the kid. Dean turned back to the fumbling young man.

"What caliber?"

"What?"

"What caliber of rifle?"

"Um... A hunting rifle. I don't know. A twenty-two, I guess."

Dean looked down and shook his head sadly, then glanced back up to the kid again.

"*If* I have a twenty-two *and* the bullets to go with it, which I'm sure you don't have, what do you got in trade?"

The kid stepped forward and pulled a leather pouch the size of his fist from his jacket pocket. He placed it on the table and then stepped back again, jamming his hands into his pockets once more.

Dean took the pouch, loosened the leather drawstring, and dumped fifteen gold coins onto the table.

He sat back and gave a harsh laugh, shaking his head at the coins.

"Boy, what in Christ's name am I going to do with gold? Jesus, tell me you're not stupid enough to believe this shit is worth anything anymore."

"It's all I've got," the kid said, glancing between Dean and the bear.

"Well, I ain't got no rifle, not one that works anyway, and you ain't got shit to trade." Dean waved his hand at the coins. "Take your gold and hit the road, boy. Here, we trade in shit people need to survive another day, and last I heard gold doesn't burn or chew so well."

"Can't you give me anything for them?"

"I wouldn't trade day-old squirrel turds for gold, boy. Go find a dentist. Maybe he'll give you something for them. Other than that, go on and get the hell out of here."

The kid stepped forward and scooped the coins back into the pouch. He stuffed the pouch back into his pocket and turned to leave.

"Come back when you've got something someone might actually want," Dean called after him, "like bullets or chocolate. And knock next time, goddammit, or I just might blow your fool head off. A shotgun I do have."

The kid left quickly without looking back.

"You can be a nasty old bastard when you want to, you know that?" the bear said, grinning.

Dean made a scoffing sound. "What in the hell am I going to do with gold, take up dentistry? That's all that shit's good for nowadays, and there's a hell of a lot more gold layin' around than dentists."

"You know he's probably a scout. That bullshit about wanting a rifle was just so he could get a look around in here."

"Yeah, I know," Dean said with a sigh. "Goddamn raiders. Bunch of fuckin' thieves is all they are." He took a long pull on his beer and then said, "Probably with that Mankato group."

The bear frowned. "Mankato group?"

Dean grunted a short laugh and shook his head. "Jesus, Bear, you need to poke your head out of the woods more than once or twice a year; see what the rest of us humans might be up to."

"Guess I'm not that interested in people anymore."

"Well, if you weren't out killing bears and screwing coyotes all the time, you'd know there's a pretty big group of survivors over in Mankato now, close to a hundred people, maybe more. I hear they've even got electricity and some working vehicles."

"No shit?"

"No shit."

"So why haven't you packed up and moved over there? Sounds like a place you could really ply your trade."

"'Cause I also hear it's some kind of a military dictatorship. Some big raider outfit runs the place. They've been hitting all the surrounding towns pretty regular, going out a little farther every year. They ain't been here yet but I figure it's just a matter of time."

"You think that kid might be with them?"

Dean shrugged. "Maybe, maybe not. A few small raiding parties are still running around. Could be he's with one of them. Would be better if he was, anyway."

"Why's that?"

"Cause these small raiders are like coyotes. You shoot back at 'em and they run off with their tails between their legs. That Mankato group is different. From what I hear, they're big and organized, more of a militia. They do some careful scouting ahead of time. When they finally hit you, it's fast and hard. They take everything – food, fuel, weapons, sometimes even people."

"Doesn't anyone fight back?"

"Sure, but all that does is get more people killed and your houses burned. Any survivors they leave have just one choice; either stay and starve come winter or make their way to Mankato. If you've got the skills and you don't mind thievin' and killin', maybe you join up with the militia. Otherwise, you join the civilians. I hear the militia eats better."

The bear sighed. "And you wonder why I live in the woods and steer clear of people." He leaned back in his chair. "So, what are you going to do if that kid was a scout and he returns with his friends? You have any weapons?"

"Got my shotgun, and I sure as hell ain't gonna let them take everything I have without a fight."

"You want me to hang around?"

Dean shook his head. "You go on back to your woods. Terrorize some more furry little woodland critters. I'll get with Roland and the others and we'll decide how to handle this. Kid didn't look smart enough to be with Mankato anyway. Probably some small scavenger outfit is all. They show up in town here, we'll send 'em packin'."

The bear raised his growler and tipped it to Dean.

"You just be careful, old man. Don't go dying on me, at least not until you've taught Roland everything you know about leather work."

"Thanks for your concern. It's touching. But don't worry about me. You just finish your beer and take that damn coat of yours with you when you leave. It's stinkin' up my whole shop something awful."

***

It was late afternoon and the snow had stopped falling by the time Erik stepped out of Dean's shop. He left his duffel bag behind, figuring the old man could add it to his collection of items for possible trade. He could easily find another when he needed one.

After closing the door, he stood and gazed out over the thick layer of new snow. The kid's tracks went off to the east, in the direction of Mankato. Erik doubted the kid would be walking to Mankato today. The city was a good fifteen miles away. With the snow slowing him down, the kid wouldn't make it halfway before sunset. It stood to reason he and whoever he was with must have a camp out there somewhere, probably in the grove of woods about two miles to the east.

He continued to stand outside Dean's shop for a few minutes, staring at the distant grove until he spotted the thin tendril of white smoke rising from the trees. Well, at least they were smart enough to keep their campfire small and not announce their presence. And with only the one small campfire, it couldn't be a very large group, probably just three or four men.

He considered if he should go pay the distant camp a visit, maybe convince them that raiding the village of Jordan would not be in their best interest. But that would take him two miles east and well south of his own camp along the river north of here. It would also mean him getting more involved than he really wanted to be.

Best to let Dean, Roland, and the other villagers handle it. They had weapons and something worth defending here. They would make short work of a small raiding party. The village didn't need his help. Besides, it seemed whenever he got involved with people, something bad always happened.

He turned and headed north.

The village of Jordan was a widely spaced collection of two dozen or so houses and buildings in southwestern Minnesota. The storm twenty years ago had probably wiped the entire town out, save for maybe one or two people and a few animals. But its location at the intersection of two roads and a set of railroad tracks, along with the lack of any other nearby towns, made it a natural gathering place for any survivors coming in from the surrounding farms. Jordan was now the home of eighteen men and women, along with a couple dozen pigs tended by Roland, some goats and cattle, and a few dozen chickens – a handy trading post for those passing through, but also a tempting target for any raiding party that might stumble upon it.

He walked easily through the new snow, much easier and quicker than most people, with his coat open and his staff in hand. Nearly twenty years of hiking the hills and forests all up and down the Midwest, in good weather and bad, had conditioned and strengthened his body. He couldn't remember the last time he had ever been tired or out of breath.

As he passed by the houses on the east side of the village, he was aware of the faces in the windows watching him. Thanks to Dean's big mouth all those years ago, everyone in this village and others he sometimes passed through knew him as "the bear." He was an enigma to them – a lone, mysterious figure in a bear-skin coat who roamed the forests and hills of western Minnesota and beyond. He never intended to become any sort of legend, but he did have to admit it worked in his favor. People might duck into their houses and peek out their windows when he came through town, but at least they tended to leave him alone. That was fine with Erik. Except for Dean, Roland, and a few others he might occasionally trade with, Erik preferred as little contact with people as possible.

Leaving the village, he continued north across a small field that had once grown corn, beans, oats, or some other crop. Now it was a patchwork of snow-covered saplings and thick brush. He'd heard Roland and a couple of the other villagers trapped for rabbits out here.

The woods began where the field ended, descending into the river valley a few hundred yards past the tree line. As he made his way through the woods to his camp along the riverbank, he was well-aware of the occasional snap of a twig or thump of a clumsy boot about twenty or thirty feet behind him. It was the kid, moving from tree to tree and being about as stealthy as a blind cow.

He guessed the kid had been scouting the village earlier and saw him come in from the woods. When the kid left Dean's, he'd headed east for a ways before circling back and waiting for Erik to leave. He probably thought someone camping alone in the woods would be an easy target to rob of his pistol, knife, and whatever else Erik might have.

Stupid kid.

Reaching the bottom of the hill, he followed the river upstream to the northwest, checking the lines he'd set earlier wherever the bank was free of ice. By the time he reached his campsite, he had two channel catfish of respectable size and a pretty hefty carp. He rekindled his campfire, sat down on a length of log, laid his staff on the ground at his feet, and set about cleaning and preparing the fish for smoking.

As he was slicing the last of the fillets into thin strips, the kid came up behind him. Erik heard the cocking of a small pistol, likely a .22 or a .38.

"On your feet, asshole," the kid growled, trying to sound bigger and tougher than he was.

Erik ignored him. He could tell by the kid's voice he was less than twenty feet behind his right shoulder. He finished slicing the fillet he was working on, wiped the Bowie knife across his leg, and carefully slid it back into its sheath.

"Are you fucking deaf, old man? Get on your feet."

Old man? He took his pouch of salt and sprinkled it generously over the fillets. Now the kid was getting rude. He would admit he looked a little rough and worn, but he was only thirty-five for Christ's sake. He turned the fillets over one by one and began to salt the other sides.

The kid stepped closer and shifted a little more to his right.

"Jesus Christ, you dumb fuck. Leave the goddamn fish alone and get on your feet or I'm going to blow your fucking head off." His voice had gone two pitches higher. He sounded more frustrated than menacing.

Erik gathered up the salted fillets and moved them to the rack he had set up above his campfire, laying them out deliberately one by one. He heard the kid step closer again, now about ten feet away.

"Goddammit, I'm going to shoot you. Get up and turn around."

If the kid had any bullets in that pistol, and if it actually worked, he would have shot already.

He took a handful of the small chunks of green hickory he'd cut up earlier and placed them in the fire. They began smoking almost immediately. Leaning forward, he placed one hand on his staff while blowing into the coals.

The kid, angry as hell now, stepped closer and moved to position himself next to the fire so Erik could see how dangerous he was. He was holding his pistol straight out in front of himself with one arm.

Before the kid could order him to get on his feet again, Erik brought his staff swiftly up and around, cracking the kid on the side of his head. The kid went down but still held onto his pistol. Standing, Erik swung the staff around again in a single, fluid arc and brought it down hard on the kid's forearm. There was a crack of bone, a scream of pain, and the gun fell to the ground.

Erik took a step forward and picked the pistol up. He brushed the snow away and examined it. It was a .38 snub-nose revolver. As the kid's screaming oscillated up and down like some annoying alarm, Erik checked the cylinder and saw that it was empty – no big surprise there. Bullets were in short supply these days and ten times more valuable than the gun itself.

He tossed the pistol into the river and sat back down to watch his fish.

The kid's screaming turned to crying and whimpering as he squirmed in pain on the ground, trying to cradle his shattered forearm with his good arm.

"You broke my arm. Goddammit, you broke my arm. Oh shit... God."

Erik used a stick to move a few of the coals and hickory chunks into better positions so the smoke could reach the strips on the edges of the rack.

The kid continued to cry and curse, rolling from side to side, occasionally kicking his heels into the ground, as though that would somehow lessen the pain in his arm.

"God. Oh god it hurts. Jesus."

Without looking up from his fish, Erik growled, "Boy, get the hell out of here and go cry somewhere else before I throw you into the river too."

The kid scrambled backwards a few feet on his butt and then struggled to his feet, still cradling his arm. "Goddammit. Oh Jesus. Goddammit. Where's my gun?" He looked back and forth across the ground. "Where the fuck is my gun?"

Erik hung his head and let out a sigh. He was running out of patience with this idiot. He had never needlessly killed anyone, but it was getting close to being needed here for just a little peace and quiet.

"Did you throw it in the river? Goddammit, you got no right, you sonofabitch."

He picked his staff up and turned to the kid, taking a step forward.

A look of fear shot through the kid's eyes. He stumbled backwards, almost fell, turned, and then ran down the riverbank, stumbling, tripping, cursing, and whimpering in pain all the way.

Erik watched him until he was out of sight. Even when he could no longer see the kid, he could still hear him whimpering and crashing through the trees.

After a few minutes, he sat back down to tend to his fish, enjoying the quiet of the riverbank and surrounding woods once more.

***

"Where the hell is that moron?" Baker growled, standing up and staring off in the direction of the village.

"Probably got lost," Cody replied, poking at the campfire with a stick. "Stupid shit probably can't follow his own tracks back in the snow."

Baker moved away from the fire and began pacing back and forth, casting glances toward the village every time he reversed direction. They were camped under the trees on a small hill east of Jordan. A wide, flat field of snow with occasional clumps of trees lay between them and the village. Somewhere beneath all that snow was an old road.

"Shit. It's getting too late. We're going to have to stay out here all night."

"So, what if we do?" Vern replied. He was sitting on a log a few yards from the fire, leaning back against a tree with his long legs out in front of him and his arms folded across his chest. He had an old, brown, felt cowboy hat tipped forward on his head, hiding all but his square chin.

"It's fucking cold, that's what," Baker said. "And it's going to get a whole lot colder as soon as that sun goes down. I didn't dress for this shit."

"We all have our lessons to learn, don't we?" Vern replied.

"I'll teach that little shit a lesson of his own is what I'll do." Baker cast one last look to the west and squatted down by the fire again, rubbing his hands together. He was a short, thick man with a square face, short graying hair, and a beard he liked to keep trimmed so close it looked more like five o'clock shadow.

Vern was a little pissed at the kid too, but he wasn't going to show it. You had to appear in control and in charge at all times, even when everything around you was going to hell. If you didn't want your men questioning your every decision, you had to act like you knew this shit was going to happen all along and you've already got a plan for it.

"We'll go first thing in the morning," Vern said with what he hoped sounded like an unconcerned sigh. "Kid gets here or not; we'll go in the morning. Just get some more wood for that fire, enough to last the night."

"But we won't know the layout," Cody said. "We won't even know if that old man's shop is worth the trouble." He was taller and leaner than Baker. Though he was also a little younger, with a round, youthful face, he was already losing his hair in the front. Even his beard was beginning to show a few strands of gray mixed in with the reddish brown.

"It's worth it," Vern said from under his hat. "Guy's been trading in that town there for years. Word is he's got a lot of crap in that little shop. We'll go in the morning."

Baker and Cody seemed to finally accept the situation and the plan. They fell silent, squatting by the fire, each taking turns poking at it with sticks.

A half-hour later, the kid came stumbling into camp, not from the west but from the north. He shuffled to a tree next to the fire and fell against it, breathing heavily. His hair was matted with sweat and his face was pasty white. He was holding his right arm with his left and he looked to be in a lot of pain.

Baker and Cody both stood and turned at the kid's arrival. Vern simply looked up and tipped his hat back, revealing the sharp angles of his narrow, clean-shaven face and his dark, piercing eyes.

"Jesus, where the hell have you been, Willy?" Baker demanded.

Cody moved to the kid and looked at his arm. He turned to Vern. "I think his arm is broken."

Vern hesitated, sighed audibly, and then got to his feet. Baker and Cody moved aside as he joined them at the tree. He took hold of Willy's arm by the wrist and carefully pushed up his sleeve. Willy winced in pain. The kid's forearm was swollen to almost twice its normal size and was turning a dark shade of purple.

"Can you make a fist?" Vern asked.

Willy took a deep breath, held it, and grimaced with effort. New beads of sweat appeared on his forehead. His fingers twitched a little but didn't close. He let his breath out heavily and shook his head. Vern let go of his arm and Willy went back to cradling it with the other.

"It's broke alright," Vern said. "What the hell happened?"

"Some guy. Hit me with a stick."

"Who? That old man in the shop?" Cody asked.

Willy shook his head. "Big guy. Mountain-man looking fucker. Wears a long fur coat made of bear skin or something. Hit me with a stick the size of a goddamn tree."

Baker looked at Vern, frowning. "The bear? What in the hell would he be doing around here?"

"He roams all over from what I hear. Probably trading some skins or something." Vern looked at Willy. "What did you do to piss him off?"

"That's bullshit," Cody said. "The bear's a myth, like bigfoot or the abominable snowman. Ain't no one I've ever met ever seen him, not with their own eyes anyway. It's just a bunch of stories idiots make up to try and scare each other."

"He's real," Baker said. "Too many people talk about him. Always the same description."

"Have you ever seen him?" Cody challenged. He looked at Vern. "Have *you* ever seen the bear?"

"Who's the bear?" Willy asked in a pained whimper.

"He's the one who broke your arm," Vern said. "Consider yourself lucky. From everything I've heard about him, you cross the bear, you usually don't live to tell about it."

"Fucking ghost stories," Cody grumbled.

"What I want to know," Vern continued, looking back to Willy, "is what in the hell you did to piss him off. You were supposed to be scouting that old man's shop. And where is your gun?"

"I didn't know who he was, okay?" Willy whined, his face scrunched in pain. "He had this big gun in his holster and a big knife…"

"You tried to rob the bear?" Baker looked both shocked and impressed. "Damn, kid! You've got some balls."

"That's not balls," Vern said. "That's shit for brains." He turned back to Willy. "Was the bear in the old man's shop?"

Willy nodded.

"What was he doing there?"

"They were just sitting there, drinking beer, I think. There were some deer hides on the table. I guess he was trading with the old man."

"So, you were in the shop," Cody stated. "Is it worth hitting tomorrow?"

Willy nodded. "He's got a lot of stuff in there. Hides, food… Guns too, I think. At least a shotgun."

"What happened with the bear?" Vern pressed.

Willy shook his head. "I followed him down to the river. I thought I could get his gun and knife. I didn't know who he was. I've never even heard of the man."

"You heard of him now?" Baker asked sarcastically, poking Willy's arm.

Willy howled.

"Did he take your gun?" Vern asked.

Willy wiped his nose on the sleeve of his good arm and nodded again.

"Is this guy going to be a problem?" Cody asked. "I'm not saying he is the bear – probably just some big local guy – but could he screw us up for tomorrow?"

Vern considered it. "No, I don't think so. We'll go ahead as planned. If it is the bear, and I'm betting it is, he's done trading now and he'll stay down by the river. From everything I've heard about him, he heads north in the spring. He'll probably be heading out soon anyway. He doesn't like being around people unless he has to."

"What about the old man and the rest of the village?" Cody asked. He looked at Willy. "You didn't piss anyone else off, did you? Let everyone know we're coming?"

Willy shook his head weakly. He looked like he was about to pass out.

"We're good," Vern said. "At least he didn't fuck up in town. We'll hit the old man's shop first thing in the morning and then head out like we planned. We don't want to show up in Mankato empty handed." He nodded to Baker and Cody. "You two get some more wood for this fire and break us out something to eat." To Willy, he said, "You sit down and try not to screw anything else up. You ain't worth spit with that arm. Shit, I don't know if Mankato will even let you in now. You'll stay here and wait for us. Maybe when we get to Mankato, and if they let you in, we can find someone to take a look at your arm."

While Baker and Cody went into the trees to find more dry wood, Willy made his way to the campfire and sat down next to it, looking pitiful and sorry for himself.

Vern had no sympathy for him, but he did have to admit that this idiot kid was the first person he'd ever heard of who had crossed the bear and lived. That was a drinking story he was sure the kid would play up again and again with much exaggeration over time once he realized how lucky he was to still be alive.

He had never seen the bear himself. Like most everyone else, he had only heard the stories, like how the man killed a grizzly with his bare hands and now wore its skin as a trophy, and how he would ambush moose and deer in the woods and kill them with a single swipe of that big stick he carried. Sometimes he just punched them with his fist. Some people claimed he slept with wolves, could even talk to them. The stories changed from town to town, depending on who was telling them. But the one rule he had always heard about dealing with the bear, the one rule that always remained constant, was the rule the kid had just learned the hard way.

You do *not* fuck with the bear.

***

Erik took a piece of fish from the rack and bit into it. It was firm and not too dry, with a smoky, salty taste. Unlike raw or fully cooked fish, this meat would last for several days. In this cold, it might even be good for a week or better.

He put most of the fish jerky into a deerskin pouch and then sat back against the log, chewing another of the pieces and staring into the fire.

That damn kid had to have been a scout. His lame-ass attempt to trade gold coins for a rifle… clumsy but telling. He was likely a new recruit for that group camped beneath the trees east of Jordon, and they were breaking him in by sending him out on scouting runs. His attempt to rob Erik had just been some amateurish mistake, trying to make a score on his own. He was probably getting his ass chewed out by his partners right now, if he had made it back to his camp yet.

He took another piece of fish and tore a chunk off with his teeth. Shit, he probably should have killed the kid. A lame raider was a worthless raider. He had heard of raiding parties that sometimes killed or abandoned their wounded, considering them a liability. Kid better hope he's not in with a group like that.

But when he did make it back to his camp, he would report on what he'd seen at Dean's. It was too late today for any kind of raid, but tomorrow… Erik shook his head, still staring into the fire. Tomorrow they'd probably hit Dean's little shop for sure.

His gaze shifted to his new boots. Besides Dean having stitched him up and saving his life all those years ago, everything he was wearing had been made by that cranky old bastard. He owed Dean much more than a few free deer skins and rabbit pelts.

Dean had assured him that he and Rolland could handle the raiders with the rest of the villagers. Erik was sure they could if the kid and his partners were a small raiding party doing their own thing. But what if the group the kid was with wasn't a raiding party? What if they were scouting for the militia in Mankato? A few weeks ago, he'd come across a small town to the southeast, big enough to where it should have been home to at least a handful of survivors. Instead, the town was abandoned. Houses were burned and all the food and supplies were cleaned out.

Small raiding parties didn't hang around long enough to burn houses – they were strictly hit and run. Now he wondered if Mankato could have been behind that attack. Dean said they scouted ahead first, and if the villagers resisted, the militia would kill most everyone in town and then burn their houses to the ground.

As much as he hated getting involved, he couldn't let a militia or band of raiders hit the old man and the town.

He sighed, knowing he'd already come to a decision. He knew where the group was camped. Whether they were little more than armed scavengers or scouts for Mankato, maybe he could stop this before it went any farther.

He took a handful of fish strips out of the pouch and put them into his coat pocket. Pulling the drawstring of the pouch tight, he tied a loop of rope around it and hung it from the limb of a tree, out of the reach of hungry raccoons, bears, or whatever else might catch scent of it. Other small deerskin bags of smoked venison and dried fruits and vegetables hung from other limbs. It was a lesson he'd learned the hard way a long time ago. Keep your provisions out of reach and away from where you sleep. He'd survived one encounter with a hungry bear. He didn't want to see if he could survive another.

His food secure and his campfire banked for the night, Erik set off following the kid's tracks down the riverbank. It was already evening but the sky was clearing to reveal the stars and a bright half-moon. Following the kid's prints in the new snow wasn't even a challenge.

MAY 4

Searing pain brought Willy out of another short, fitful dream. It was the umpteenth time he'd rolled over onto his broken arm. He'd gotten only an hour's worth of decent sleep all night.

He sat up, sucking his breath through clenched teeth. God, he had never felt such pain. He almost felt if he could hack his arm off to make the pain go away, he would do it in a heartbeat.

As the immediate, searing pain slowly gave way to the more familiar, constant throbbing that made him want to throw up, he regained his focus enough to glance around the camp. The sun was just coming up, sending long shadows across the new snow. A few bright stars were still visible in the deep blue sky to the west. Vern, Baker, and Cody were asleep in a tight circle around the remains of the campfire. Thin tendrils of smoke were rising lazily into the cold morning air.

He was about to try laying back down to see if he could catch another five or ten minutes of sleep when something caught his eye on the east side of camp.

He stared, squinting, his eyes still blurry from his fitful sleep, trying to see through the deep shadows thrown off by the surrounding trees in the growing light. There was something there, silhouetted against the morning sun. It looked like the thick trunk of an old tree, a little over six feet in height, but it seemed oddly shaped for a stump. It looked more like...

Willy felt his gut clench and he lost all thought of the throbbing pain in his arm. He kicked out at Cody, who was lying closest to him.

"Cody!" he hissed. Guys! Get up!"

Cody grumbled and pulled his bedroll up closer to his chin.

Willy grabbed a handful of snow and flung it at the man's face.

Cody sputtered and sat up, flinging his hand out to ward off the snow. "Jesus! What the fuck are you doing?"

"Over there," Willy hissed, pointing to the edge of camp. "It's him."

Vern and Baker, awoken by Cody's shouting, also sat up.

"What the hell is going on?" Vern growled.

"It's the bear," Willy said urgently, jerking his head toward what he had mistaken for a thick tree stump. "He's here."

Vern and Baker immediately got to their feet, followed by Cody. Willy struggled against the pain in his arm and finally pushed himself to his feet.

They stood around the remains of the campfire and stared at the large, silhouetted figure at the edge of their camp. He didn't move. He didn't say anything. He just stood there, watching them. The end of his staff was planted in the snow in front of himself. He had both hands on the staff and his feet shoulder-width apart.

Vern thought he looked like some kind of sentinel one might encounter guarding the gates of Hell.

"What is he doing?" Baker asked, barely above a whisper.

"Shit," Vern said. He quickly glanced around and confirmed what he thought he was seeing lying in the snow at the bear's feet. "He's got all our guns."

The others quickly glanced around.

"Goddammit," Baker said, glaring at Cody. "You were supposed to be on watch."

"Quiet," Vern commanded, not taking his eyes off the tall, silent figure.

So, this was the bear. He had heard the stories about the man but had never seen the legend himself. Like most people, he'd only half-believed in the bear's existence. But now there was no doubt. The bear was most definitely real and he was here, now, standing there like some goddamn grim reaper deciding on whether or not he was going to mow them all down.

What did he want? He could have easily killed them all in their sleep. Instead, he had taken their guns and set up watch over their camp, waiting patiently for them to wake up. The brazen confidence that implied was a little unnerving.

"Hey!" Vern called to him.

No response.

He took a couple of tentative steps toward the imposing figure, cocking his head slightly, looking for some reaction. The bear remained silent, impassive. Vern took a few more steps. He heard his men moving up behind him, following a couple of steps behind. When he had approached to within ten feet, the bear finally moved, shifting his feet a little and lifting the end of his staff out of the snow. He held it at an angle across his chest – an unmistakable warning not to approach any closer.

Vern and his men stopped.

"You shouldn't just walk into someone's camp unannounced." Vern said. "It's dangerous."

The bear said nothing.

Vern was close enough now to see some of the bear's features. But he wished he could see more than just the man's eyes through that thick beard and long hair. He couldn't read any expression at all. But those eyes... they were cold, hard. There was no fear in them at all. Even outnumbered four to one, the easy way he held that staff and those cold, uncaring eyes said there would be no doubt as to the outcome of this encounter. The bear would walk away. As for Vern and his men, whether they lived or died depended on what they did in the next sixty seconds.

"What do you want from us?"

"Leave," the bear said. "Now. Don't come back. Ever."

Before he could consider a reply, Vern heard Cody speak up from behind him.

"Why should we? We're here on legitimate business. We came here to trade in that town."

Vern mentally groaned. That jackass was going to get them all killed.

The bear cocked his head slightly. His expression changed from cold and hard to curiously amused.

"What do you have to trade?"

Cody turned to Willy and slapped him on his good arm. "Get it out."

Willy winced in pain and shook his head, indicating it was a bad idea.

Cody slapped him harder. "The gold, man. Come on."

Grimacing, Willy reached into his pocket and brought out the pouch of gold coins. He handed them to Cody. He shifted his eyes to the ground, avoiding looking at the bear.

Cody tossed the bag forward. It landed at the bear's feet next to their guns.

The bear reached down and picked up the pouch. He opened it, dumped the coins into his hand, and put them into his pocket without examining them. He then reached into another pocket, pulled out a handful of something, and put whatever it was into the pouch. He tossed the pouch to Vern.

"Trading's done," the bear said, no longer appearing amused. "Now you leave."

Vern opened the pouch and looked inside. Despite what he was seeing, he breathed a sigh of relief. Maybe they would get out of this alive.

"Yeah, well what about our friend?" Cody said, indicating Willy. "You busted his arm up pretty good. Maybe they've got a doctor in that town."

"Jesus, Cody," Baker growled. "Would you shut the fuck up?"

The bear reached under his coat and drew out the biggest knife Vern had ever seen.

"No doctor there," the bear said. "But we can take care of that arm right here if it's bothering him."

Willy's face went two shades whiter than it already was. A dark stain appeared in the crotch of his pants as his bladder let go.

"Jesus, no! Hold on," Vern said quickly. "Like you said, the trade's done. It's all good. We're leaving. Just let us pack up our shit. You won't see us again."

The bear continued staring at them for a few seconds before sliding the knife back into its sheath under his coat. As he did so, Vern saw the pistol in his belt. It looked like a large caliber revolver. He had no doubt that it was fully loaded.

Without another word, the bear turned and walked out of camp, heading west toward the village. He didn't even look back once.

Cody raced forward and grabbed his pistol out of the snow. He slapped the snow off, examined it, and then turned to the others.

"Fucker took the bullets and packed the barrel with snow."

Baker walked up to him. Without warning, he hit Cody as hard as he could with a right cross to the jaw. Cody spun backwards, out cold before he hit the ground.

Baker turned back to Vern, expecting to be admonished.

"Why the hell didn't you do that two minutes ago?" Vern asked. "Jesus, what a moron."

"So, what'd he give us?" Willy asked, nodding to the pouch in Vern's hand.

Vern tossed the pouch to Willy, who managed to catch it with his one good hand.

Willy undid the drawstring with his teeth and looked inside. "What is this? Fish?"

"Seeing as we're still alive," Vern said, "and all it cost us was a handful of worthless gold coins, I'd say we got the better end of the deal. Now let's get this shit packed up and get out of here before he decides to come back." He nodded to Cody, still lying unconscious in the snow. "And if that dumb sonofabitch doesn't wake up by the time we leave, his ass stays here."

***

Erik flicked his thumb and watched the coin arc through the air, flashing morning sunlight with each flip. It plopped into the snow and disappeared beneath, joining a dozen of its brothers under the blanket of white. He idly wondered if maybe in two hundred years or so, if civilization ever climbed back up to where it had been before the storm and gold was worth something again, maybe some lucky bastard would find them and thank some new or old god for his good fortune.

He was sitting on a small hillock, surrounded by a grove of cottonwood saplings, less than a mile north of the raider's camp. He had headed west toward the village until he was out of their line of sight and then circled back to keep an eye on them. Now he raised the small pair of binoculars he carried with him to his eyes again.

The raiders had broken camp about an hour ago and were now trudging single file through the snow, heading east. They were following the old east-west road that led from Jordan to the highway and then on to Mankato, but Erik could see no sign of a vehicle of any kind. Part of him was disappointed. He hadn't seen or even heard of a working vehicle in twenty years. It would have been interesting to see one again. But then another part of him was relieved. Dean had said Mankato used vehicles. If these guys were hoofing it, they probably didn't belong to any organized militia.

In addition to their lack of a vehicle, Erik had been far from impressed by their campsite. When he'd entered it last night, he had looked for any evidence they were planning a big raid, as opposed to a hit-and-run scavenger operation. They had a couple of backpacks and shoulder bags in their camp but nothing that would have let them carry away any serious amount of loot. They had been ill-dressed for this weather and their weapons had been as unimpressive as the kid's unloaded pistol. He'd found three more pistols, only one of which was fully loaded, and a single thirty-caliber rifle with three shells in it.

He lowered his binoculars, convinced now that they weren't heading for any hidden vehicle. These guys were not part of any militia – not the fighting part of one, anyway – and they sure as hell weren't successful raiders. They were just piss-poor scavengers on the down-hill slide. Even their food supplies were meager – a single can of beans, a few cans of cat food, some dried roots of some kind, and a couple boxes of stale pasta.

He considered if maybe scouts were low on the totem pole in a militia. That might account for their meager supplies and pathetic clothes and weapons. But low on the totem or not, he doubted if an organized militia of the type Dean described would have sent four men this far out in the snow without a vehicle or at least a horse to ride back into town.

He reached into his pocket and felt the few remaining gold coins and the handful of bullets he'd unloaded from the scavengers' guns. The coins, of course, were worthless, but maybe he'd give the bullets to Dean the next time he saw him. None of them were .22 or .44 caliber, so he had no need of them.

He'd left the scavengers unarmed and pretty much defenseless, but that was their own damn fault. If they'd just come into the village and asked for help, he had no doubt the people of Jordan would have given them food and shelter for the night, maybe even let them stay until the weather changed.

Hell, maybe he should have let them try to raid Jordan. Dean, Rolland, and the other villagers would have made quick work of them. A quick death would be better than starving or freezing out here in the snow, which was very likely if they didn't make it to Mankato or some other shelter in the next day or two.

He pocketed his binoculars, picked up his staff, and headed back north to his campsite along the river. He figured chances were good he would not see the four would-be raiders again, but he also figured he would hang around the area for another few days, just to be sure.

MAY 11

McClain sat on the edge of his bed, slowly bringing his knee up as high as he could and then lowering it back down and straightening his leg, working the stiffness out of his hip. It hurt like hell but he knew it would hurt even worse if he didn't go through this morning ritual. That goddamn bullet from back in Elk River... A piece of it was still in there, buried deep in the joint. Saundra had done her best, but there was only so much she could do without any real medical equipment.

After a few more knee-hip flexes, he carefully stood up. With the help of his cane, he took a few trial steps. Not bad. Not great but not bad. The cane helped take the weight off his hip joint. Once he got moving around for the day, the stiffness would work itself out and the sharp pain would eventually subside to a dull ache.

God, what he wouldn't give for some real aspirin or ibuprofen, but the supply of pain killers and most other medicine had run dry over ten years ago. He'd tried drinking a tea made of willow leaves Sara brewed for him once. She claimed it contained a natural kind of aspirin. It worked but it also gave him diarrhea. If he had to choose between the pain and a day of sitting on the toilet shitting his guts out, he'd choose the pain any day.

He made his way to the window and stood looking out over the old college campus. He was stark naked but he wasn't worried about being seen from the windows of the apartments across the street. Most were unoccupied. The civilian population of Mankato lived in the houses and apartments farther east and to the north. The campus itself was reserved exclusively for Pierce's militia. While McClain was not actually a member of the militia, he did serve as a kind of liaison between the militia and the civilians and was therefore required by Pierce to live on campus.

It was late morning and the sun was already well over the trees and rooftops to the east. It looked like it was going to be another sunny day, probably a little warmer than yesterday but still jacket weather. After that last snowfall a little over a week ago, it had been gradually warming up. Most of the snow was already melted. If the weather held, the grass would finally begin turning green again in two or three weeks. It had been another long, hard winter and he was looking forward to warm weather and budding trees again.

The distant rumble of trucks and the rattle of big diesel engines to the north brought him out of his daydreaming of spring. That would be Orlando's group returning from St. Peter, a town about fifteen miles north. McClain glanced in the direction of the approaching trucks even though he knew he wouldn't be able to see them. He hadn't expected this latest raiding party to return until tomorrow or maybe the day after that. Either everything went well, or it went very badly.

He turned from the window and crossed the room back to his bed. Sara was still asleep. As he began pulling on his clothes, she mumbled something and turned over onto her side, pulling the blankets up to her chin. She was ten years younger than him, with long, dark hair and dark eyes. Her real name was Sarada. She was a student over here from India back before the storm and was one of the original handful of Mankato survivors.

He leaned over and kissed her lightly on the cheek. She had been with him for nearly seven months. Before McClain, she had been with one of Pierce's top lieutenants who recently fell out of favor. And before that, she had been with another of Pierce's men. She was just one of several women Pierce employed to keep him informed of what his men were doing or talking about. McClain didn't mind. It meant Pierce still considered him important enough to warrant bedding a spy with him.

He finished dressing and then went downstairs for a quick breakfast before leaving the house. He tried to be present every time the militia returned from one of their raids so he could mentally inventory the haul. He didn't agree with the militia or their tactics, but he wanted to be sure at least a reasonable portion of the haul made it to the civilian population in town. Pierce tolerated this oversight only because he knew the civilians of Mankato outnumbered his militia three to one. If they became hungry or dissatisfied, they could easily overrun his little empire and throw his tinpot-dictator ass out into the cold.

One of the big military trucks, a deuce-and-half, was already being unloaded when McClain arrived. A dozen men were carrying cases of food and supplies recently "liberated" from St. Peter into one of the old administration buildings that had been converted to storage. A second two-and-a-half-ton truck held several head of livestock crowded into the back – sheep, goats, cows. These would be unloaded later down at the old campus stadium.

McClain noted fresh bullet holes in the side of the first cargo truck and a shattered windshield. Two of the pickup trucks also showed signs of having been in a recent firefight.

Pierce was talking with Orlando and Vlad next to the truck that was being unloaded. Orlando, a five-foot-ten, burly Hispanic man with a ponytail and Fu Manchu mustache, was Pierce's second-in-command and led all the big raids. Vlad, a six-foot-four, strongly built Norwegian with blonde hair hanging past his shoulders, was Pierce's most ruthless raider. He fancied himself a Viking warrior of old. Except in the most extreme weather, he wore a fur-lined leather vest to show off the Celtic knot tattoos running up both of his thick arms. He generally manned one of the fifty-caliber machine guns that were mounted in the backs of two of the pickup trucks. But for up close and personal work, he favored the double-edged battle ax with a leather-wrapped handle he had stuck in his belt.

Also with Pierce was Jules, a six-foot-seven black man of enormous size. McClain wasn't sure if he was Pierce's actual bodyguard or if Pierce kept him close simply for intimidation purposes. Jules rarely spoke but, when he did, it was with a deep, rumbling, mellow voice. Jules spent most of his time standing next to Pierce with his arms crossed over his chest, implying instant death for anyone who dared get too close even though he never carried a gun. There was no shortage of rumors about his past – former death-row inmate, former Secret Service agent, former hitman for the mob. But no one really knew anything for certain about the big man.

"Captain," McClain greeted Pierce, giving him a half-assed salute and dropping it before Pierce could return it – a subtle insult the "captain" had never caught onto. He hated calling Pierce "Captain." It was a rank the little shit had bestowed upon himself after taking over from Colonel Bates thirteen years ago. Pierce was no more than a former low-level postal worker who had become a scavenger after the storm and then a raider until finally murdering his way into leadership of the militia. He was a scrawny little man with Hitler hair and small, mouse-like eyes. But like any good fascist, he was conniving, manipulative, and ruthless – a dangerous man to be on the wrong side of politically.

Pierce cast his usual disdainful glance down at McClain's cane.

"Expected you'd be here sooner, McClain. Leg bothering you this morning?"

"No more than usual," McClain said, ignoring Pierce's snide tone. He nodded to the men unloading the truck. "Looks like your men did well."

"Not really. Didn't get shit for food. A few weapons, supplies..." He nodded to the other truck. "Fucking livestock. Might as well slaughter 'em all right now so we don't have to feed them."

McClain feigned surprise. "St. Peter? I thought your scouts said they had a bigger population, maybe twenty or thirty people and a couple good stores of supplies."

"They did," Orlando said. "I scouted it myself last week. But they knew we were coming. They hit us with an ambush as soon as we entered town." He snorted derisively. "Nothing we couldn't handle, but then they burned their supply stores before we could get to them."

"Lookouts?"

"Pretty fast response time for lookouts," Pierce said. "More like they were ready for us and had their defenses in place before we even arrived."

"Maybe your reputation precedes you," McClain said dryly. "Remember Owatonna last year? They fought back pretty hard too. And Faribault and Waseca before that. Could be some survivors from one of those towns made their way to St. Peter and warned them to be on their guard."

"Anything's possible," Pierce said. "But I doubt it. How did they know exactly *when* we were coming? Pretty hard to believe they've had an ambush in place and ready to go since last year." He shook his head. "No, this was a well-planned defense, with a fallback plan to burn the supplies and leave nothing for the enemy. More likely someone got word to them."

"A spy," Vlad grunted.

"A traitor," Pierce countered. "But it doesn't matter in the long run. If someone is tipping these towns off to our plans so they can fight back, all they're doing is getting a lot of people killed for nothing." He turned to Orlando. "In a few days, I want you and a couple of men to go back in there. I assume you left survivors?"

Orlando shrugged. "A few."

"Good. Stay out of sight and watch them. I'm betting they didn't burn all their supplies. They probably just moved most of it to another location. When you find where it is, finish the job."

"Jesus," McClain said. "You're going to just slaughter them?"

Pierce looked at him, his brows furrowed. "Well maybe whoever is running around warning these towns when we're coming can now warn them about what happens when they resist. This isn't a game, McClain. We're in this for survival."

He turned to Vlad. "In the meantime, I want you and Parsons to take half a dozen men and go to that town west of here – Jordan, I think it is – the one those men that arrived last week said they came from. Take one of them with you since they've already scouted it. I want Parsons to lead. You'll back him up but let him make the calls."

Vlad frowned. "Parsons?"

"He's not very experienced," McClain said. "Might be better to put someone else in charge."

"Hardly your fucking concern, McClain," Pierce snapped. To Vlad he said, "Parsons has been on the sidelines long enough. I want to see how he does on point."

Vlad gave a slight, noncommittal shrug but didn't say anything.

"Jordan didn't sound that promising," Orlando said. "A little over a dozen people at best and not much in supplies – livestock mostly. Hardly worth our trouble."

"That's not important this time," Pierce said. "What's important is that they know who's in charge around here. They've been sitting there right under our noses this whole time and we didn't even know they were there. Then a handful of half-starved scavengers stumble upon them and the locals send them packing with their tails between their legs. Hell, they might even think those dumbasses were with us. That's the kind of defiance that can spread to other towns and cause us problems down the road, problems like St. Peter."

"They said it was the bear that chased them out," Orlando said. "Jumped them in their camp. They said only the one scout even got into town."

"The bear," Pierce scoffed. "Might as well blame it on the boogeyman. They just don't want to admit that a bunch of pig farmers kicked their asses."

He turned and looked at Jules, who had been standing next to him like an immovable oak tree the entire time.

"How about you, Jules? Do you think this *bear* is real?"

Still staring straight ahead, Jules gave only a slight shrug. "Don't know," he stated in his smooth, baritone voice.

Pierce turned back to Vlad. "You and Parsons roll in there like any other raid. But stay alert. We don't know what really happened there. If anyone gives you any trouble, you bring the hammer down."

Vlad grinned, nodding as his hand went to the battle ax in his belt.

"And if you see anyone hanging around that village wearing a bear skin," Pierce continued, "I want you, personally, to take him out. Make it public. We don't need any local heroes or bullshit legends giving people ideas."

MAY 13

Dean had often thought if anyone could be accurately described as a "portly fellow," it was Roland. At six-foot-two and over three hundred pounds, the man was as round as he was tall. With reddish-blonde hair and hands the size of Christmas hams, he wasn't so much fat as he was just plain big. Quiet and thoughtful, often pausing to consider before speaking, he defied both the jolly fat man and big bully stereotypes.

Dean had set him up with a workbench next to his, where the big man could tinker with his collection of broken firearms, swapping parts back and forth and occasionally fabricating new parts, finally putting Dean's old metal and woodworking tools to use again. When he wasn't tinkering with cracked rifle stocks, broken trigger springs, or worn firing pins, Roland helped out with the repair and sharpening of farming tools. He had even started learning the leather trade.

Although Dean was glad to finally have the help, it was becoming apparent he was going to need either a bigger shop or a smaller apprentice. Squeezing between Roland on his work stool and a rack of spades, shovels, hoes, and rakes, Dean made his way to a barrel of hickory ax handles at the front of his shop. He had worked these last year. He selected one to replace the handle of a splitting ax that had come in yesterday. He was turning back to his workbench when he heard a sound from outside that he hadn't heard in twenty years.

He hesitated, listening, wanting to make sure he wasn't hearing things. He glanced at Roland, who had turned around on his work stool and was staring to the front of the shop.

"Trucks?" Roland asked.

"It ain't goddamn Santa Clause," Dean said. He went to the window and looked out just as a camouflage-painted pickup truck skidded to a stop right outside the door. He saw two other trucks, one with a machine gun mounted in the back, roar past as they headed farther into town.

The doors to the pickup flew open and two men got out. The big one, with long hair past his shoulders, was wearing a leather vest and had tattoos running up and down both his thick arms. He had a rifle slung across his back and a short-handled, double-bladed ax stuck down in the wide leather belt around his waist. The other man was only a third the size of the first – short, squat, and covered in more body hair than Dean thought possible on a human. This one also had a military-style rifle, either an M-16 or AR-15 Dean guessed.

The big one pulled the ax from his belt as he strode to the door of the shop. The little one hurried to join him, holding his rifle across his chest like some ugly, miniature, storm trooper.

"Shit," Dean growled. He glanced at Roland again, who was just standing up from his work stool. "We've got raiders." He lifted the ax handle in his hands like a baseball bat and stepped to the side of the door just as it crashed inward under a heavy kick from the big man's boot.

Not waiting for the men to enter the shop, Dean swung the ax handle as hard as he could around the corner of the doorway, at where he guessed the man's head would be. What would have been a skull-crushing blow against a man of normal height only caught this one on the shoulder, thudding heavily but not even causing him to hesitate.

The man stepped inside. With a single, backhand swipe, he sent Dean stumbling back against the heavy wooden table off to the side of the door.

The little troll-like man rushed in after the big one, stepping in front of him and spraying bullets in an arc across the workshop's ceiling. He was cackling in a crazed, high-pitched laugh.

Dean's head was swimming from the big man's blow and his vision had gone cloudy. He leaned against the side of the table, trying to keep his knees from buckling.

"Where's the bear?" the big man roared.

Roland, who had gotten only half-way across the shop before being stopped by the spray of bullets, held his hands up, palms out toward the man.

"Whoa, there. Calm down, big fella. The bear isn't here."

The man turned to Dean. "Where is he?"

"At your house, fucking your sister," Dean growled.

No sooner had the words left his mouth than the man stepped over and grabbed Dean by the front of his shirt. As easily as Dean might lift an infant, the man hauled Dean off his feet and threw him over the table.

Dean hit the floor hard. His head spinning, he looked up just in time to see the big man's boot coming toward his face. Stars exploded in his head and then, mercifully, everything went black.

***

Erik sat on the side of the hill, his back against a tree, quietly watching the creek bed below. A small .22 caliber lever-action rifle lay across his knees. He remembered when Sergeant Ortiz had given it to him back at the mansion in Elk River. Ortiz had said it would come in handy for hunting small game like rabbits and squirrels, and even larger game if his aim was good enough. Corporal McClain had added that it could also be used as a sniper rifle if it ever came to that. It had never come to that, but the simple little rifle had helped keep Erik in fresh meat over the years.

He let his gaze move slowly up and down the wide creek bed, seeing the trees and brush on either side but not really focusing on anything in particular. It was a good scanning technique he'd learned for detecting even the smallest movement of a squirrel or rabbit, or the earliest appearance of a deer deep in the woods.

It also gave him time to ponder some of life's great mysteries, like why in hell he was still in this area, hanging around in the woods below Jordan and not twenty or thirty miles north by now.

Following the creek south would bring him to the river and the same campsite he'd been using for nearly two weeks. He hadn't stayed in the same place for more than three or four days since that farmhouse down along the border nearly twenty years ago, where he and April had been trapped for weeks by an early, heavy snow.

Shit. If that damn kid hadn't followed him and tried to rob him, he would have been long gone by now. Sure, that pathetic group of scavengers would still have tried to raid Jordan, but Erik was sure Dean, Roland, and the other villagers would have had no problem dealing with them. Erik wouldn't have even known about it until he came back this way next year and Dean regaled him with the story over another beer or bottle of wine.

He shifted his position against the tree a little, keeping his movement to a minimum lest a deer see him before he saw it.

Despite his decision to abandon humanity and never again form more than a passing relationship with anyone, he had screwed up and become fond of Dean and that dumb little village. There were even nights when, just before falling asleep, he caught himself wondering what it would be like to be part of a community again, to share dinner and conversation with a few friends. And now here he was, hanging around, trying to ignore it but still worried either the scavengers he had driven off would be back, or they really were a scouting group out of Mankato.

Movement in the trees down the hill about fifty yards away caught his attention. It was a deer, still behind a grove of saplings, moving forward slowly, browsing for green shoots and bobbing its head up every few seconds to scan for danger. Thoughts of Dean and possible vengeful raiders were immediately pushed into the background as Erik focused his attention on the doe.

He waited until her head was down and then he began to slowly raise the rifle to his shoulder, pausing whenever the deer's head bobbed back up. He eased the hammer back. By the time the doe stepped clear of the saplings, he had the rifle sighted on her, his finger lightly touching the trigger.

He was just beginning to put pressure on the trigger when he noticed additional movement behind the saplings. The doe looked back and then walked forward a little more. A fawn stepped out into the open. It was only a few weeks old, with white spots still running down its back. A second fawn appeared behind it – twins.

Erik kept the rifle sighted on the doe, his finger still on the trigger, but hesitated. If he killed the doe, the fawns may or may not survive to summer. If they found their way to a herd, they would probably be adopted by the other does and they would survive. If not, it was a sure bet wolves, coyotes, or a bear would have them for lunch before the week was out.

He continued tracking the doe as she moved forward and the fawns followed. After a while, he took his finger from the trigger and slowly lowered the rifle. Might as well let her go. This wasn't the only deer in the woods and there were plenty of squirrels and rabbits too. Besides, he had enough meat to get him by for at least another week. And when he came back this way next year, there would be two additional grown deer for him to hunt.

He leaned back against the tree to wait for the doe and its fawns to move far enough up the creek bed where he could safely stand and leave without alerting them to his presence. He didn't want to spook them. As long as they felt this area was safe, they would be back. And they may bring others with them.

A rapid series of pops came from over the hill behind him. The doe's head bobbed up. She stamped her hoof. Her fawns froze in place.

Forgetting the deer, Erik stood and looked up the hill. The sound of automatic weapons was unmistakable. He heard another short burst and then a longer one. The sounds were coming from the direction of Jordan.

"Shit."

He started up the hill as fast as he could. Behind him, the doe and her fawns were already long gone.

By the time he reached the top of the hill, the sounds of gunfire had ceased. Over the trees, he could see black smoke rising from the southeast corner of Jordan, where Dean's shop stood.

Erik moved quickly through a narrow stretch of trees and came into the village from the north. He could hear truck engines and men shouting. There was another quick burst of gunfire. Staying low and behind the trees and houses as much as possible, he moved toward the center of town, where all the noise was coming from. Several cows and pigs, loosed from their pens, passed him as they fled toward the woods.

Easing around the corner of a house, Erik could see a group of seven villagers standing together in the street. They were being guarded by two men armed with automatic rifles. A third man stood in the back of the pickup truck next to a fifty-caliber machine gun that was mounted in the bed. Erik recognized one of the guards on the road as one of the raiders he had rousted a couple of weeks ago, a shorter man with a closely-trimmed beard.

Another pickup was parked in the middle of the road closer to Erik. Next to it lay a dead cow. A little beyond the cow was a dead dog. At least there were no villagers lying dead in the street yet.

A tall, thin, redheaded man was directing two other men as they moved down the street in Erik's direction, kicking in doors, shouting, and dragging people out into the street at gunpoint.

Farther down the road, where Erik could see the smoke and flames billowing up from Dean's shop, a third pickup truck was approaching. As it skidded to a stop next to the redhead, Erik saw Roland and Dean in the bed of the truck. Roland had his arm around Dean's shoulders. Dean was slumped over, his face swollen and bloody.

Two men got out of the truck: a small, troll-like man holding an M-16 and a large man with long hair who looked like some kind of Viking warrior on steroids. The Viking had an M-16 slung across his back and a large, double-bladed ax stuck down in the wide leather belt around his waist. As the troll approached the redhead, the Viking went to the back of the pickup, dropped the gate, and dragged Roland and Dean out of the bed.

Erik couldn't hear what the troll was saying to the redhead but it looked like they were arguing. The redhead finally turned away and walked toward two men who were pushing an old woman from her house. The troll turned back to the Viking and made an "off with his head" motion across his neck.

The Viking forced Dean to his knees and then backhanded Roland as he tried to intervene. Another man who had been rousting people out of their houses stepped forward and forced Roland back at gunpoint.

The redhead turned back to the scene on the road and shouted angrily, "Stand down!"

The Viking ignored the redhead and pulled the ax from his belt. Erik quickly raised his rifle and sighted in on his head. Just as he was about to pull the trigger, the man who was holding Roland at gunpoint took a step back, right into his line of fire. Erik pulled the trigger anyway, shooting the man in the back of his neck.

Before the man could hit the ground, Erik wheeled and sprinted around the back of the house to the other side. As he peered around the corner, he could see the men in the street all gawking at the man twitching on the ground. He wasn't dead yet but soon would be.

Everyone had gone silent and none of the raiders had reacted yet. The Viking was looking around, standing with his ax in one hand and the collar of Dean's coat in the other. Erik aimed and fired. The Viking jerked back, releasing his grip on Dean but not his ax. Erik quickly ducked behind the house again and sprinted to the next house.

Now, there was a sudden flurry of shouting, running, and shooting back at both places Erik had been, rapid bursts of gunfire tearing into the houses and trees. The redhead was shouting the loudest, trying to direct his men, but they either were not listening or they couldn't hear him over the sounds of their own gunfire.

From a third position, Erik sighted in on one of the two men in the street guarding the villagers. As soon as he'd killed one, the villagers quickly turned on the other and overpowered him – the raider Erik had recognized. They knocked him to the ground, took both his rifle and the one from the dead guard, and ran for cover. Two stayed behind a few extra seconds to deliver some vicious kicks and blows to the downed raider.

Erik didn't wait to see the outcome. He reversed direction and ran back to one house down from his original position. As he ran, he could hear engines starting up and the redhead yelling over sporadic bursts of gunfire for his men to regroup on the trucks.

As he peered around the corner, Erik was shocked to see the Viking just twenty feet away, grinning and striding directly towards him, battle ax in hand. He had spotted Erik and was moving to intercept him. Blood was flowing from the left side of his head. Erik had either only grazed him or the man's skull was too thick for the little .22 caliber bullets to penetrate. Erik guessed the first but the second was not out of the realm of possibility.

He dropped the rifle and stood up. Taking a wide stance, he pulled his pistol from his belt, thumbed the hammer back, and took careful aim, intending to put a hollow-point .44 magnum slug between the Viking's eyes. Even if his head was made of steel and filled with concrete, at this range, the forty-four would blow it clean off.

One of the trucks suddenly raced up between the Viking and Erik. The troll had his rifle out the passenger-side window. He was shouting something unintelligible and spraying bullets wildly in Erik's direction. Erik ducked back behind the house as bullets thudded into the wood and a window shattered. A second truck pulled up and skidded to a stop. The redhead shouted at the Viking to get in.

Automatic weapons' fire began coming from down the street. The villagers who had grabbed the guards' guns were shooting at the fleeing pickup trucks. As the third truck rolled by, Erik saw one of the men in the bed firing back at the villagers with the .50 caliber. The raider, having survived his beating by the villagers, was driving. Erik fired twice, knocking the machine-gunner out of the back of the truck with the second shot.

The Viking got into the second truck and it accelerated down the road, following the other two. Erik fired after it, blowing the back window out but not hitting either the redhead or the Viking. The Viking turned and looked back at Erik through the shattered windshield. He flashed a sneering grin and lifted his ax as if to show Erik what lay in store for him the next time they met.

He watched as the trucks disappeared down the old road, heading back in the direction of Mankato. When they were out of sight, he turned and walked toward the center of town where several bodies lay in the street and the villagers were slowly coming out from under cover to assess the damage.

The men and women of the village moved aside as Erik passed among them up the center of the road. Most were standing and talking amongst themselves. A couple of the women were crying. None of the villagers had been killed, though three or four appeared to be injured. Apart from the dog and cow, the three dead bodies lying in the street were raiders and no one was giving them much attention. Erik figured they would later be dragged out behind the houses and burned. At least, that's how he would dispose of them.

Dean and Roland were nowhere to be seen so Erik headed for Roland's house, which was closer than Dean's. He let himself in and found Dean lying on a couch in the living room. An older woman with white hair was sitting next to him on a chair, gently dabbing at Dean's forehead with a wet towel. She looked up at Erik's arrival and gave a startled, "Oh!"

Roland appeared just then from the kitchen with another towel in his hands.

"It's okay, Mom. He's not one of them." He crossed over to his mother and helped her to her feet. "Why don't you go in the kitchen and heat up some soup? It would probably do him good."

The woman nodded and handed Dean her towel. "That's a good idea." She cast a quick, nervous glance back to Erik and then hurried off to the kitchen.

"You tend to scare the women-folk, you know that?" Dean said from the couch after she'd gone. "Probably 'cause you're so damn big and ugly." Both of his eyes were black and his nose was broken and swollen. He also had swelling on his cheekbones, two deep cuts on his lower lip, and thick bandages on both hands.

"Well, they didn't beat the grumpiness out of you," Erik said, turning the woman's chair around and sitting in it so he could look over the back at Dean. "But I've seen dead coyotes in the woods that looked a damn sight better than you look right now."

"That's about how I feel," Dean said, closing his eyes. "That big sonofabitch has iron in his fists. Hits like a goddamned truck."

"Good to see you, Bear," Roland said. "If you hadn't shown up when you did…"

"Just blind luck I was still in the area," Erik lied, "and close enough to hear the gunfire. How much damage did they do?"

"Burned the shop is all," Roland said. "Roughed a few people up and chased some of the livestock off. You stopped them before they could do anything more. That, and I don't think their leader, that tall redheaded guy, really wanted to kill anyone. Good movement on your part, by the way. They thought they were being hit by two or three snipers."

"God damned Mankato," Dean said, his eyes still closed. "Figured they'd sniff us out sooner or later."

"What the hell did you do to piss 'em off?" Erik asked. "That big Viking was ready to chop your head off."

"Hit him with an ax handle," Roland said. "The shop was the first place they hit – kicked in the door as soon as they got there. The Viking came in first and Dean just couldn't resist taking a swing at him."

"Like whacking a goddamn oak tree with a whiffle bat," Dean said. "Bastard didn't even feel it."

"I think you got lucky he decided to just beat you up a bit," Roland said. "That little troll with the machine gun kept dancing around, trying to get a clear shot at you. I managed to get in the middle of it all and draw their attention. I guess they didn't want to beat on me so much, but that little troll bit me on the arm. Then they set fire to the shop before they dragged us up here."

"They didn't loot anything from the shop before torching it?"

Roland shook his head. "Didn't take anything. Not from the shop or the houses. I think they were just hell-bent on terrorizing us, but you drove them off before they could tell us why."

Erik looked down at the floor, considering the raider he'd recognized. Glancing back up at Roland, he said, "It's probably my fault. A couple of weeks ago, a scout came into the shop while I was there. Dean probably told you about that. He followed me to my camp. I drove him away but then followed him later. There were four of them camped out east of here. I sent them packing but it appears they've joined up with Mankato now – I recognized one of them. That must be how they found you."

"Shit, I already guessed something like that," Dean said. "That big, tattooed guy asked about you. Wanted to know where you were. I said something nasty about his sister and he threw me into a wall."

"It's not your fault," Roland said to Erik. "I'm sure Mankato would have found us sooner or later."

"I could have killed them. I had the opportunity, but all I did was chase them off."

Dean opened his eyes again and looked at Erik.

"Like Roland said, it's not your fault. From what I've heard, Mankato's been pushing farther and farther out every year. They would have found us this year or next." He laughed a bit and then grimaced at the pain. He took a breath. "Hell, at least you gave them a taste of their own medicine today, showed them that not everyone is going to just roll over and take their crap."

"That's what I'm afraid of," Erik said. "They may not like the taste of their own medicine. They may be back to punish you for what I did."

"They might," Roland said. "Or they might not. Could be they won't think we're worth the trouble now – too much loss for nothing gained.

And it's not like we're sitting on a stockpile of supplies here. We don't have anything they want."

"They don't necessarily know that. But, either way, it might be a good idea to prepare in case they come back. Decide what you're going to do, fight or run."

"We'll do that," Roland said, nodding. "I'll get everyone in town together and we'll figure something out."

Erik stood up.

"You're not going to do anything stupid, are you?" Dean asked. "Go back to your woods, Bear. This shit's not your fault and you shouldn't get involved. Just look us up when you come through again."

For the second time that day – the second time in his life – Erik lied to Dean.

"You're probably right. Maybe I'll just head north like I should have done a couple of weeks ago." He reached down and squeezed Dean's shoulder. "You just get back on your feet, old man. When I come through this fall, I'll have some hides and maybe some other stuff for you – get you back in business again."

"I won't take charity," Dean protested.

"It won't be. It'll be on credit, like when you helped me out all those years ago."

He turned to Roland.

"Looks like you're going to be blacksmith and cobbler for a while. I hope this old coot has taught you something more than just foul language and bad attitude. In the meantime, I think I saw some of your hogs headed for the woods north of here. If I see them again, I'll try to shoo them back this way."

Roland nodded. "That's okay. I'll round 'em up later." He reached out and shook Erik's hand. "Don't worry about us. We've survived this long and we'll keep on surviving. I look forward to seeing you again in the fall."

Erik gave a final nod to both men and then turned and walked quickly out of the house. With long strides, he headed north out of town toward the woods, ignoring the side-glances and hushed whispers of the villagers.

***

It was one of those rare times when McClain could not read Pierce's expression. He knew from experience that was bad. It meant the little fascist was seething with rage inside but was controlling his outward emotions to the point of looking almost bored. It also meant he wasn't going to let whatever was pissing him off go. At some point – today, tomorrow, maybe next week – he was going to direct all that fury in a single instant against someone or something.

"Why did you call a retreat?" Pierce asked calmly, directing the question to Parsons. He was seated at his desk in what must have once been the old on-campus house of the college dean or president.

Parsons was standing at-ease in front of the desk, his feet apart and his hands clasped behind his back. On either side of him were Vlad and Bean, a short, squat, troll-like man with big ears and a hooked nose. He was the hairiest man McClain had ever seen.

McClain was the only other man besides Pierce who was sitting. He had chosen an overstuffed chair off to the side and next to the windows. He normally wouldn't have joined this meeting, but for some reason Pierce had ordered his presence.

The ever-present Jules stood as he always did, next to Pierce with feet apart and arms crossed over his massive chest. He stared straight ahead, ever stoic, ever ready.

"We were taking fire from several directions," Parsons stated flatly so it didn't sound like an excuse. He was staring at the wall over Pierce's head. He seemed to be struggling to keep his acne-scarred face from betraying his nervousness. "There were three, maybe four snipers. They killed three of my men in a matter of seconds and wounded two more. We took damage to the trucks. In my judgment, we had been outmaneuvered. I didn't want to hand the village a total victory so I called for a roll-out. I take full responsibility."

"By roll-out, I assume you mean retreat," Pierce said.

Parsons hesitated before replying. "Yes, sir."

Pierce stared at him but said nothing for almost a full minute. Finally, he directed his attention to Vlad.

"How many snipers did you see?"

"One sniper," Vlad replied. "It was the bear. I saw him running behind the trees and houses, changing his position quickly."

"The bear," Pierce said, pondering on the name. "How do you know it was him?"

Vlad gave a slight shrug. "The way he dressed, the way he looked." He paused before stating almost proudly, "He was not afraid of me."

"Baker confirms it," Parsons said. "He says he recognized the man."

Pierce fixed his gaze on Parsons again.

"So, one man fooled you into thinking he was many. One goddamned stump-sitter killed three heavily armed, experienced men and chased you out of town with a fucking small caliber rifle."

"When he shot one of the guards," Parsons said, a little too quickly, "the villagers overwhelmed Baker and grabbed both of their weapons. Our machine gunner was dead. We were sitting ducks in the middle of the road."

"Johnson was killed *during* your retreat," Pierce corrected him, referring to the machine gunner.

Parsons didn't reply.

Pierce leaned back in his chair, his gaze drifting across everyone in the room. He let his last words hang in the air for a long while. Finally, he glanced back to Parsons and gave a slight nod to the door.

"Get the hell out of here. You're dismissed."

Parsons turned and walked quickly out of the room. After he'd gone, Pierce turned and jabbed his finger at Vlad.

"I want that dumbass out front on the next raid, understand? And the next after that. I want his ass front and center until he grows a pair of balls or someone shoots him in the head. Jesus, what a fuck-up. He should have opened up with that fifty-cal after the first shot, laid waste to the whole goddamn town."

"Are we going back in?" Vlad asked.

"No. Not now. Not yet anyway. We've got something more important coming up. Orlando will fill you in. But once we're done with that, we're going to turn that little shit-stain of a town into a pile of ash and bone. There won't be so much as a field mouse left alive in Jordan once we're done with it, much less a fucking bear."

Vlad grinned and nodded. Bean, the hairy little troll next to him, chuckled.

"You two take some R&R. I'll let Orlando know you're off the clock for now but don't go too far. We've got a major score coming up and I'm going to want every swingin' dick rested, alert, and ready to roll out quickly. You're dismissed."

After Vlad and Bean were out of the room, Pierce leaned back in his chair and swiveled to face McClain, putting his hands together behind his head.

"How about you, McClain? You used to be a soldier. Would you have turned tail and run?"

Given the same situation, McClain thought, he would have, if for nothing else than to save the lives of his men. But he told Pierce what he knew the little megalomaniac wanted to hear.

"No, I would have fallen back into a defensive position until we could locate the shooter and take him out with overwhelming firepower. That's a standard sniper technique – shoot and move. Never fire from the same position twice in a row. It was simple inexperience that led Parsons to mistake the man for multiple shooters. Could be this 'bear' has some military training."

"I seem to remember," Pierce said, "you said something about Parson's inexperience earlier. But I don't think he mistook anything. It was pure cowardice. I think he took the sniper as an excuse to bug out of there as fast as he could run. I debriefed his men earlier. He had no intention of putting the fear of God into that village. He thought he could go in, cuff 'em around a little, speak a couple of harsh words, and they'd fall in line." He shook his head. "I really thought Parsons had more balls than that."

"Maybe he's not cut out to lead."

Pierce scoffed. "That's putting it mildly, but we'll fix that." He paused and appeared to consider something before changing the subject.

"You ever heard of a town up north called Belle Plaine?"

McClain felt his stomach clench a little at the name but kept a neutral expression.

"Yes. Colonel Bates and I passed through there sixteen or seventeen years ago. A little farming community, if I remember right. Hardly more than a dozen or so people. Not much bigger than Jordan."

"Not so little anymore. As you know, I sent Orlando and some men back up to St. Peter last week to have a look around. Turns out the place is deserted now, a ghost town."

"Not surprising," McClain said, wondering what the connection was. "You killed most of them and took whatever supplies they didn't burn."

"They had quite a bit squirreled away according to Orlando. He found the empty stores. They didn't really burn much. It's like we figured. Someone got word to them ahead of time about our raid and they were prepared for us. The buildings they burned were mostly empty. Looks like a few of their braver men sacrificed themselves in the ambush to fool us into thinking they were defending a hoard. It gave the rest of the town time to scoot out the back with the bulk of their supplies."

"So, what does this have to do with Belle Plaine? You don't think that's where they went, do you, the ones that scooted out the back? That's quite a ways to be hauling a town's worth of supplies."

"I *know* it's where they went. After finding St. Peter empty, Orlando and his men checked some of the farms in the area. You know there are always a few squatters in these isolated farms, people who don't want to come into the city and are hell-bent on making it on their own."

"Like Jordan."

"Exactly. And Orlando found a couple of farmers who confirmed it. Just before our attack, they saw a small caravan of people and horses pulling a lot of wagons and carts, heading north on the highway."

"That's got to be better than forty miles, and that highway is in pretty bad shape. Are you sure they made it that far?"

"Orlando tracked them. He saw signs all along the way where they stopped to rest or camp. He followed them all the way up to Belle Plaine."

McClain thought it over but couldn't see any way of dissuading Pierce from what he was obviously planning.

"This is the 'big score' you were talking about?"

Pierce nodded, a shit-eating grin on his face.

"It can't be that big," McClain said, grasping at one last straw. "There were only a handful of survivors there when the Colonel and I went through. They were farmers. Add to that the survivors from St. Peter and you've got what, a couple dozen, maybe three dozen people?"

"Try a couple hundred," Pierce said, still grinning, "or close to it. And they're entirely self-sufficient. Orlando and his men gave it a quick scout, keeping well out of sight, of course. They've got livestock, fields, greenhouses, grain stores... everything but the most important element for survival."

When Pierce didn't elaborate, McClain prompted him. "Which is...?"

"Guns, McClain. Weapons. Oh, they may have a few for hunting, but Orlando saw absolutely no sign of any defenses. None of the villagers he saw were even armed. Hell, he said a small troop of girl scouts armed with slingshots could walk right into that place and take whatever they wanted. I'll bet it's been ten years or more since they've seen a raider or even a scavenger. They probably think they're perfectly safe and secluded up there."

"Leaving them wide open for your little band of marauders."

Pierce scowled. "You would rather starve, McClain? What about all your civilians here? Do you want them to starve, freeze to death this next winter?"

He didn't reply, still very much aware of Pierce's bottled-up rage over the fiasco in Jordan.

"Anyway, you're wrong," Pierce continued. "Yes, we're going to Belle Plaine, but not to raid it, not this time. When Orlando reported back on what he'd seen, I thought about it and decided it's time we start thinking bigger. When you find a plum tree this laden with fruit, you don't cut it down."

"So…," McClain said, trying to figure out what Pierce was getting at. "What's the plan?"

"I thought that would be obvious. I intend to take Belle Plaine. No more raiding. This time, we're going in to conquer and occupy."

MAY 15

Erik sat in the trees on a low hill west of the athletic field, watching with binoculars as trucks and men went into and out of the old football stadium. The activity wasn't constant, but it was enough for him to see the little raiding party that hit Jordan the other day was a small part of something much larger. This outfit was big and well-armed. They had half a dozen working trucks, including two or three big diesel cargo trucks – deuce-and-halves, Erik thought they were called – and a couple of Humvees. At least two of the pickup trucks had machine guns mounted in the back.

Maybe they had started out as raiders and scavengers a long time ago. But now they were, as Dean had called them, a militia. He estimated there were more than twenty raiders in the group, with another fifty or sixty civilians in the town to the east. He hadn't seen the Viking yet, or the troll or any others he might have recognized.

He swung his binoculars to peer into a line of trees north of the stadium. A large black man was sitting under one of the trees in a meditative position. He had his hands on his knees and his eyes were closed. He'd been sitting like that for nearly an hour. Erik wondered if he was a raider or a civilian. He was on the old college campus, which indicated he was with the raiders, but he seemed to have no interest or involvement in what anyone else was doing.

He watched the man for another couple of minutes, briefly considering maybe the man was dead, but then discarded that notion and swung his gaze back to the campus. He swept the binoculars slowly across the buildings and up and down the streets, still not sure if he was looking for anything in particular or just spying. Even if he saw the Viking, he would be too far away to shoot and he couldn't go down there and kick his ass like he wanted to. That would be like sticking his hand into a hornets' nest to try and pinch off the head of the one that stung him. How smart would that be?

As his gaze passed over what appeared to be some kind of maintenance building, he spotted a second man who seemed out of place among the rabble of raiders – an older-looking man coming out of the building and down the steps. He was dressed in civilian clothes, unlike the quasi-military outfits most everyone else was wearing, and he walked with the aid of a cane. He had a pistol on his hip. But unlike most of the other men, he did not carry a rifle.

The man reached the bottom of the steps and turned in Erik's direction, making his way slowly down the sidewalk. Erik continued watching him, feeling there was something familiar about the man but unable to quite grasp what it was.

After a few steps, the man looked up as if feeling Erik's gaze on him. It was only a brief glance and then the man looked down again to continue on his way, but it was enough for Erik to realize with a start that he did recognize the man. Corporal McClain. He was twenty years older now and had put on some weight but Erik was sure it was him. And the limp. He remembered McClain getting shot in his hip and arm when that religious cult had attacked the mansion.

What in the hell was McClain doing here? Why had he left Elk River? How was he connected to this militarized band of raiders?

He continued watching McClain until he turned up another street and disappeared from view behind a row of apartment buildings.

Lowering his binoculars, Erik considered this new development. He hadn't planned on going down into the hornets' nest. He had just wanted to get a better idea of how big this group was, what they had for vehicles and weapons, and what they were all about. But McClain's presence in the middle of it all? He had to know more. The Corporal McClain he remembered would never have been part of a raider outfit. The Corporal McClain he remembered would have used these bastards for target practice.

As he was considering his options, he heard footsteps and voices approaching from behind him and to his right. He glanced over his shoulder. Shit. It was a roving patrol, two men with rifles slung over their shoulders. They hadn't seen him yet but they would in another handful of seconds.

As he stood, Erik mentally chided himself for not having chosen a vantage point with better cover. He turned to face the approaching men and planted his staff on the ground in front of himself. He didn't want to kill them and maybe he wouldn't have to. He just hoped they had damn thick skulls.

***

Jules could feel the passing of time as the sun moved in its silent arc across the sky. He felt the warm dapples of light as they came through the branches of the tree he was sitting under and crept over his face and arms, moving in the opposite direction of the sun.

There was a field mouse at the base of a tree about twenty feet ahead of him. He could hear it rustling in the grass and leaves as it scurried back and forth. A small woodpecker had briefly alighted on a branch above his head a few minutes ago but had flitted off to the north. It was about ten trees away now, scooting up and down the trunk, pecking occasionally in search of grubs beneath the bark.

In the campus behind him, he could hear men and trucks coming and going from the stadium and moving about the buildings. McClain had come out from his secret meeting with Parsons a few minutes ago and walked south along the sidewalk before pausing and then turning east, heading to his apartment. The sound of McClain's cane on the sidewalk was unmistakable. Like many times before, Parsons would wait ten or fifteen minutes before coming out of the maintenance building and heading back to the barracks so no one would make the connection between him and McClain.

His eyes closed, Jules took in another deep breath and exhaled slowly, feeling completely relaxed and at ease but still aware of everything around him. He gave little thought to any of it, letting the sounds, scents, and sensations pass over him as effortlessly as the slight breeze coming from the south, the breeze that carried on it the scent of the bear.

He had told Captain Pierce the truth earlier. He hadn't known if the bear was real or myth, not then. But now he knew. The breeze carried on it the smell of the bear hide the man wore, the slightly pungent scent of gun oil, and even the subtle, sweet aroma of his hickory staff. The man was sitting in the trees about three hundred yards to the south, watching the activity in the campus.

He heard the clumsy footsteps and senseless babble of the two guards who were approaching the bear's position from behind. He smelled the leaves and damp earth disturbed by the bear as he stood and turned toward the guards.

Jules narrowed his awareness and focused it on the bear's position. He had little doubt about the outcome of the coming encounter. It would be quick and violent. But mostly, it would tell him a great deal about the nature of the bear and the part he may yet have to play in upcoming events.

***

It was dark by the time McClain got home from the town meeting. Between people bitching about the reliability of the generators and heated debates over how to handle the growing sewage problem, all he wanted to do was sit down, kick back, have a double shot of booze – any kind would do – and then have sex with Sara. She was into the rough stuff and liked to play the dominatrix role, but she usually held back on his account. He thought tonight he would let her off her leash, so to speak, and let her indulge her kinky side. With Pierce and his men busy gearing up for their raid on Belle Plaine, he had little to do anyway over the next couple of weeks except the occasional town meeting or social visit. Plenty of time to recover.

He took off his jacket and gun belt and hung them on the coat rack just inside the door. The kitchen light was on. Maybe Sara was already home and had made him some dinner.

He crossed through the living and dining rooms and stopped dead at the kitchen doorway.

Sitting at the little breakfast table was a large, burly man with a thick, unruly beard and long hair. He was wearing a long, heavy coat made of bear hide. Leaning against the table next to him was a heavy, wooden staff that looked like it had blood and a little hair on one end.

On the table in front of him was McClain's bottle of rye whiskey and two glasses.

The bear leaned back in his chair and looked him up and down.

"Corporal McClain. What in the hell happened to you?"

***

McClain's face showed a mix of shock and apprehension. His hand went to his side and felt for the gun he had taken off after coming into the house. Erik could tell McClain didn't recognize him.

"Sit down, Corporal."

Erik poured two fingers of whiskey into each glass and slid one across the table. When McClain still didn't move, he took a sip from his own and then regarded it as he savored the taste.

"I remember I almost gagged the first time I tasted this stuff. Guess it just takes about twenty years to develop a taste for it." He glanced back up to McClain. "I can't believe you still have a bottle left. What did you call it? The nectar of the gods?"

McClain's eyes showed surprise. "Tyler?"

Erik shook his head and set his glass down.

"Tyler's been gone a long time. He saved my life shortly after we left the mansion but it cost him his own."

"Erik!" McClain stepped forward to the chair opposite him. "Oh my god, it *is* you! You... You're... We thought you went back to Iowa."

"I did. Now I'm back here." He nodded to the other chair.

McClain slowly took a seat, his eyes not leaving Erik.

"I don't hang around people much," Erik said. "I spend most of my time in the woods west and north of here." He raised his glass. "To lost friends."

McClain picked up his own glass, gave a slight nod, and drank with Erik. As he set his glass down, his gaze flicked to the staff leaning against the table and then back to Erik.

"So, you're the one they call the bear? I'll admit, I never really believed the stories. Even if I did, I sure as hell never would have thought it would be you."

"It's just a nickname," Erik said, "given to me by the man who made me this." He indicated his coat and then glanced back to McClain. "The same old man your thugs beat up in Jordan the other day."

McClain drained the whiskey in his glass and poured himself another.

"I'm sorry about that. They're not my men. I have nothing to do with Pierce's militia or their raids. I'm just a civilian now."

Erik gave him a critical look.

"You don't live with the civilians. You're on campus here with the raiders."

"I'm... a liaison, I guess you could say. The civilian population here considers me their governor. I settle disputes, direct civil projects, make sure they get their share of food and supplies. But I don't have any authority over Pierce's men. Living on campus with them is just... convenient."

Erik sat back and stared at him. This was not the Corporal McClain he'd known in Elk River. Somewhere along the way, the young, confident soldier who had faced down a religious cult and took two bullets in defense of the mansion had become a meek, defeated, shadow of his former self. The corporal he'd known back then would have killed every one of these rat bastards, not joined up with them.

"What happened up in Elk River?" Erik asked. "How did you come to be a part of all this?"

"Things change," McClain said. "You of all people should know that. And sometimes you just have to do the best you can with what you've got and keep moving forward."

When Erik didn't say anything, he continued.

"I stayed in the mansion for a couple years after you and Tyler left. Survivors kept trickling into the city every so often and we would invite them to join us – strength and security in numbers and all that. After a while, we had about a dozen people living in the mansion and maybe a dozen more in the houses around it. It was in that second year a group of armed survivalists – five of them – attacked us. We fended them off but Sergeant Ortiz was killed. The summer after that, Colonel Bates and two other men came through town. They came down from Bemidji and were heading south. I joined up with them and we eventually found our way here. Mankato was just a small group of survivors back then, just like Elk River."

Erik frowned. "There's kind of a gap in your story there, Corporal. Why would you leave the mansion? You and Ortiz were its defenders. If Ortiz was gone, that left only you."

"Not by then. We'd taken in a small group a few months earlier, two men and three women. One of the men was this tall, good looking guy everyone called Thor because he looked like a Norse god. He was smart, self-confident, a natural leader. He and Ashley hit it off right away. I don't think it was romantic, at least not that I ever saw. It was more like they were best friends, but I suppose that sometimes changes too."

Just hearing her name brought back memories of that last, wonderful night he'd spent in the mansion, the night she'd joined him in his bed. He pushed the memory away, having learned long ago not to dwell on the past, no matter how sweet or bitter it was.

"I always thought you would be the one to finally end up with Ashley."

McClain gave a bare hint of a smile. "Don't think I didn't wish that. I tried getting close to her, but she was always just a little too far out of reach. You remember how she was. Anyway, after Ortiz was killed, she withdrew even more. The only ones she really talked to after that were Saundra and Thor."

He took another sip of whiskey and continued.

"You know it was always Saundra who ran the mansion. Her leadership just naturally extended to the growing community. By then, Ashley had pretty much become her protégé and was making more and more of the decisions. And then, of course, there was Thor. I seriously think that man could have led others into battle on the weight of his smile alone. Between the three of them, they made a hell of a leadership team. They were doing great things for the community. After a while, I felt like I was just kind of fading into the background, like I wasn't really needed anymore. So, when Colonel Bates showed up and said that he was heading farther south, I took it as a sign that it was time for me to move on."

"So, you came down here and joined up with this Pierce guy?"

"Pierce and his men weren't here yet. There were about a dozen or so people on the campus when Colonel Bates and I got here. There were a couple of mechanics, engineers, I think a chemist – the kind of smart people who come in pretty handy after an apocalypse. They had already gotten a couple of generators working again and were sitting on warehouses full of food and supplies. The colonel and I joined up with them, figuring this was as good a place as any to settle down and start rebuilding civilization. There wasn't really anyone in charge when we got here, but eventually everyone just kind of adopted Colonel Bates as their default leader.

"Four, maybe five years later, we'd grown to about twenty-five people. We were taking in survivors, former scavengers, anyone who was tired of going at it alone. It was around then that Pierce and his men showed up. I didn't like him, figured he was bad news, but the colonel always gave everyone the benefit of the doubt. He figured a person's past was his past and that people can always change for the better."

"Not always," Erik said. "Some people never change, or they change for the worse."

"I don't think Pierce changed for the worse. I think he was always bad. But he's one of those slick, sneaky types who will tell you whatever you want to hear, show you what you want to see, but all the while planning to rob you blind or stab you in the back. He's a con man of the worst kind, a true sociopath. The colonel never saw that."

"So how did this Pierce guy come to be in charge? Couldn't you do anything to stop him?"

"We got hit by a couple of small raider groups shortly after Pierce arrived. Personally, I think it was Pierce and his men who orchestrated the raids but I could never prove it. Either way, it gave him the leverage he needed to convince the colonel to allow him to form a militia, for the protection of the community, of course. A couple of months later, we began to suspect the militia was raiding surrounding communities while using Mankato here as its base of operations."

"Sounds like the perfect excuse to get rid of him."

"It was. But the colonel died before he could confront Pierce. Maybe a heart attack, maybe a stroke… maybe something else. He was found alone and he didn't have any injuries anyone could see. I think Pierce or one of his men had something to do with it. The timing was just too convenient. But I didn't have any proof."

"So that should have left you in charge."

McClain nodded. "I was at first. Still am, as far as the civilians are concerned. After the colonel's death, I tried disbanding the militia but they had grown too large and powerful by then. Pierce had spies everywhere. He still does. I couldn't make a move without him knowing it and outmaneuvering me. He and his men worked behind the scenes and got the town to appoint me as governor and himself as captain of the militia."

"Why doesn't he just take over outright? I mean, what's the point of keeping you on as some kind of puppet leader?"

"I don't know. Like I said, he's a cunning bastard and I'm sure he has his reasons. I think maybe it's just easier for him to keep me in place to handle all the mundane civilian matters so he and his men can focus on their raids."

"And the civilians just go along with this?" Erik asked. "No one cares that he's running wild out there, slaughtering people and burning villages?"

McClain sighed. "They don't want to know. Pierce keeps them fed and he keeps the generators running. It's easy to let the butcher do his work as long as you don't have to watch how your steak is prepared."

Erik leaned back in his chair, trying to understand how people could be so willfully ignorant. It sounded like, as McClain said, Mankato had started out with the best of intentions. But over time, for the sake of security and comfort, they had let Pierce turn them into little more than obedient sheep, waiting at the trough for their next feeding.

"Why don't you just leave, maybe go back to Elk River or somewhere else?"

"Believe me, I think about that every day. But, besides the fact that my leg gets worse every year, I'm in a unique position here, as pointless as it might seem on the surface. Although I'm technically a civilian and not part of the militia, I am privy to most of their plans. Not a bad place to be if you're looking to mitigate damage and maybe save a few innocent lives."

"What do you mean? You're working against him?"

He shrugged. "I do what I can, little things here and there, like getting word out to the villages or towns Pierce and his men intend to raid. If I can't stop the slaughter, at least I can provide a little warning, maybe give people enough time to defend themselves or get the hell out."

Erik felt a bit ashamed for having thought McClain would have willingly joined up with a raider outfit. But working behind the scenes to sabotage their efforts? That sounded pretty damn dangerous, especially considering what he was learning about this Pierce character.

"Sounds like you're playing with fire in a room full of dynamite," Erik said. "What happens if they figure out you're the fly in their oatmeal?"

"I'm sure I'll be executed, probably publicly." McClain shrugged. "I've come to terms with it. I've got a couple other people I work with. We all know the risk and we've decided it's worth it."

This sounded more like the man Erik had known back at the mansion, someone who was willing to risk his life for others. He didn't envy McClain's position but at least he understood it now. He finished the drink in his glass and pushed his chair back.

"It's been good to see you again, Corporal. I just needed to know you weren't working with these bastards. If I'm ever back this way, I'll try to look you up, though I'm pretty sure Pierce has a bounty on my head by now." He stood and picked up his staff. "By the way, you'll find a couple of guards out by the trees southwest of here. They're not dead, but if you have ice, they're going to need a lot of it. Maybe a few stitches too."

"Are you heading north?"

Erik nodded.

McClain leaned forward. "Can I ask you to do something for me? You don't owe me anything and I'll understand if you say no. I can try to find someone else to do it if you'd rather not. But Pierce is keeping a close eye on me and my men right now so it would be best if we laid low for a little while."

Erik hesitated, thinking. A part of him said he should decline, just leave now and don't get any more involved. But another part of him said the least he could do for McClain after all this time was spare another few minutes and listen to the man's proposal.

He leaned his staff against the table again and sat back down.

McClain refilled both of their glasses.

"It's not dangerous, but there is a little bit of a time element to it."

"You want me to get word to some town that Pierce is coming," Erik guessed.

McClain took a sip of his whiskey and gave a slight nod.

"Have you ever been through a town about forty or fifty miles north of here called Belle Plaine?"

"It's possible. I don't ask the names of the places I pass through."

"You'd remember it if you had. It's a farming community right off highway 169. Hell, you and Tyler probably passed through it on your way home twenty years ago, but it would have been much smaller then. Anyway, there are almost two hundred people there now from what I hear, mostly farmers, on the southwest side of town. They're completely self-sufficient – no scavenging. When Colonel Bates and I came through there, it was nothing more than a handful of people growing gardens and tending a few animals. It's grown up quite a bit since then. There was an older woman in charge. Kate, I think her name was, but everyone called her Belle. She might still be there."

Erik lifted his glass and took a sip. He didn't remember the place and he'd never heard of a survivor community that large. Up to now, Mankato was the largest community of survivors he'd come across.

"Ever since Pierce has been in charge here, I've kept quiet about Belle Plaine," McClain continued. "I'd hoped it was too small and too far north for him to pay any attention to it. It's a good, peaceful community with hard-working people just trying to make new lives for themselves. If there's any hope left for humanity and civilization, it's Belle Plaine. It's where I've often thought about going back to if I ever leave this place."

"Sounds like the garden of Eden, version two-point-oh," Erik said. "How did Pierce find out about them?"

"A couple of weeks ago, Pierce attacked St. Peter, just a little north of here. One of my men got word to them and a lot of the people evacuated ahead of time. Unfortunately, Pierce sent some of his men back to St. Peter on a follow-up raid and they tracked those who had left up to Belle Plaine."

"You want me to warn them." Erik shook his head. "Sounds like too many people to evacuate. Are you saying you want them to fight? Do they have any weapons?"

"I don't think they have any defenses, none that Orlando reported anyway. He didn't even see anyone carrying a gun. And I know they have no idea what's coming their way. You saw what happened in Jordan. That was one of my men in charge of that raid – not his choice but he couldn't decline without raising suspicion. But that's why they didn't massacre everyone and burn the village to the ground."

"The redhead?"

McClain nodded. "Parsons. Unfortunately, Pierce doesn't have confidence in him anymore and he's being watched closely. But what could have happened in Jordan is just a taste of what Pierce will bring to

Belle Plaine. He's decided to conquer the town, not just raid it and leave. He's going to roll in fast and hard in a kind of blitzkrieg attack. It'll be bad any way you look at it. Even though Belle Plaine has the numbers, Pierce has the firepower. If they resist, it could turn into an outright slaughter."

Erik frowned. "You want me to tell them not to resist, to just lay down and accept their fate?"

"I just want you to warn them, let them know what's coming. The people who evacuated out of St. Peter should help you convince them how dangerous Pierce is." He leaned back and sighed. "Maybe with enough warning, they can plan some sort of defense, or maybe they can evacuate some of their people and start over somewhere else. I don't think it'll matter either way, but at least they'll have a choice."

Erik pondered it. He could warn them. That was simple enough. Impress on them the seriousness of the situation and then move on. Leave the decision to them. Despite McClain saying Erik owed him nothing, Erik reasoned he did owe him. It was the least he could do in return for the shelter and supplies McClain and Ortiz had given him and Tyler up at the mansion.

"How long do I have?" Erik asked.

"Pierce is sending a second scouting party up in a day or two. They'll be in a truck, so I don't think you'll be able to beat them there unless you leave right away. They'll park the truck a mile or so out of town, probably split up and walk in posing as random survivors to avoid raising suspicion. Or they'll watch it from a distance with binoculars. Either way, they'll spend a couple days looking it over and then report back here. After that, it's up to Pierce when he decides to move. I would say within a week or two of the scouts returning. Could be even sooner since he's already made his decision to invade."

Erik finished his drink and stood.

"I'll get word to them. You do what you can on this side to slow things down, give me time to find this Kate woman if she's still around and give her the bad news. After that, they're on their own. By the time Pierce and his men get there, I'll be half-way to Canada."

McClain stood and held out his hand.

"Thank you, Erik. I never thought I'd see you again. I honestly thought all this time that you were dead. I'm glad I was so wrong."

Erik shook his hand. "I've had more than my share of close calls. Maybe if I'm ever back this way, we can swap stories over another bottle of rye. Until then, take care and keep your head low."

He picked up his staff and turned to leave.

"Do you ever think you should have stayed in Elk River?" McClain asked. "Never left the mansion?"

Erik stopped but didn't turn around.

"I've thought about it sometimes. But I did what I had to do. I'll never regret that."

He glanced back over his shoulder.

"Goodnight, Corporal."

As he left the apartment and stepped out into the cool night air, Erik had the sudden feeling that, despite what he'd said, he would never be back this way. And he would never see Corporal McClain again.

***

Sara stood from where she'd been sitting at the top of the stairs. She walked softly down the darkened hallway and into the bedroom where she peered out the window.

So, that was the bear. She watched him stride quickly across the backyards of the houses, moving with practiced ease through the moonlit night. In seconds, he disappeared behind another house, heading for the trees to the west.

She'd had a headache and laid down in bed, waiting for McClain to come home from his town meeting, and she'd eventually dozed off. The sound of McClain coming in the front door had awoken her and she'd gotten up, intending to go downstairs and welcome him home. The voice of a stranger in the kitchen had stopped her.

She thought one of Pierce's men had come in while she'd been sleeping and had waited for McClain downstairs. But there had been confusion in McClain's voice at first and then recognition. She'd heard him call the stranger Erik, and then he'd said something about Erik being the bear. Intrigued, she'd sat down on the top step and listened.

She had heard everything.

Sara picked up her shoes and a coat, then quickly but quietly made her way downstairs and through the house to the back door. When she returned, she would tell McClain she had been out visiting with one of her friends.

This was too important to wait for morning.

MAY 17

Nature was quickly reclaiming all the roads and highways. Twenty years of unchecked sun, rain, ice, and snow had broken the pavement down to where grass, weeds, and small trees could finally get a foothold and continue the reclamation. There were places along highway 169 where the pavement had disappeared altogether, either because of washouts or where the trees and weeds were particularly aggressive.

Cody seemed to delight in the bone-jarring ride, jerking the wheel to the left and right as he steered around trees and the rusted hulks of ancient vehicles. He seemed determined to keep the four-by-four airborne most of the time as he bounced the truck over chunks of broken pavement.

"Jesus Christ, slow down, you numbskull," Baker growled at him. He was squeezed between Cody and Vern on the seat. "You bust this truck up and you're going to be the one walking back to explain it to the captain."

"Lighten up, you pussy," Baker said. "I ain't driven a truck in twenty years and I'm going to have some fuckin' fun with it."

Vern stared out the passenger side window, trying to ignore the two bickering idiots. This was not what he'd hoped for or expected when he'd joined up with Mankato. He was a raider, goddammit. He should be back with the rest of the militia preparing for the raid on Belle Plaine, not babysitting a couple of dimwits on a scouting run. If it hadn't been for that damn kid screwing up the raid on Jordan, they would have had something to show for their efforts when they'd gotten to Mankato. They would have proven their worth. Instead, all they'd shown up with were empty hands, empty guns, and a kid with a broken arm.

"Looked like a bunch of damn amateurs," Vern grumbled to himself as the truck took another jarring bump. The only good thing to come out of all this was that he was finally free of that fuck-up kid, Willy. His arm had been so badly broken it made him useless as a raider. Mankato took him in but only as a civilian. Now he was doing some menial job at the water treatment plant on the east side of town.

Baker hadn't helped their standing, either, by getting his gun taken away and his ass beaten by a bunch of unarmed villagers in Jordan.

And then, if that hadn't been bad enough, Cody had been on roving

guard duty the other day with one of Pierce's regular men when they had
stumbled upon the bear himself right in the middle of fucking town.
They had the jump on him. But did they kill him, take him prisoner, or
even chase him off? Hell, no. The bear had cracked them both
unconscious and took their guns again. Cody still had a goose egg on
the side of his head.

None of this had been Vern's doing but it still reflected badly on him
because Baker and Cody were his men. He'd brought them into town.
If shit kept going downhill like this, Vern was sure they were all going to
be relegated to sewage duty on the civilian side of town for the rest of
their damn lives.

Cody ramped the truck up over a slab of pavement, thumped it down
hard on its front wheels, and plowed through a grove of saplings.

"Whee-hoo!" he shouted.

Baker banged his knees against the dashboard when the truck landed.
"God damn it!"

Vern was just about to yell at Cody to stop using the truck as a
substitute for jerking off when he heard a small *pop* followed by a loud
bang from the front of the truck. The vehicle slewed sharply to the left
and rolled over.

The violence of the truck rolling was like nothing Vern had ever
experienced before. He felt himself being slammed back and forth in
the truck cab with Cody and Baker, like they were rag dolls in a barrelful
of bricks. It was loud, violent, and scary as hell.

When the rolling finally stopped, he found himself on the roof of
the up-side-down truck with Baker on top of him. His ears were ringing.
He was completely disoriented as he lay there gasping for each painful
breath. Grass, dirt, and broken glass were everywhere. He could smell
radiator fluid and gasoline mixing with the settling dust.

It took him a couple of minutes to finally get his bearings. He tried
to twist out from under Baker, who uttered a groan but seemed mostly
unconscious. Blood was trickling from Baker's scalp and it looked like
he'd bitten clean through his lower lip. Glancing past Baker, Vern saw
that Cody's driving privileges had been permanently revoked. The wheel
had broken off and the man had been impaled through his chest by the
steering column.

"Jesus," Vern grimaced.

He was struggling to extricate himself from underneath Baker when
the cab of the truck was suddenly filled with the screeching of metal as
the door was yanked open. He felt a pair of hands clamp down on his

shoulders and drag him roughly out of the truck.

His far-from-gentle rescuer jerked him to his feet and then slammed him back against the side of the overturned truck. Vern's head was still swimming from the crash and the sudden change in orientation made him feel like he was going to throw up. The daylight seemed unusually bright and his ears were ringing. Something in the back of his mind told him he was in shock and he should be lying down, but his rescuer had him pinned upright against the side of the wrecked vehicle.

The man who had pulled him from the wreckage pulled Vern's pistol from his belt, tossed it aside, and then stepped back. Vern swayed a bit and then caught his balance, using the truck for support. Squinting against the bright sunlight, he found himself staring into the bearded, angry face of the bear.

"What the...?" was all Vern was able to say before doubling over and puking all over his own boots.

When he was finally able to straighten back up, he saw the bear had taken another step or two back, probably to keep from getting puked on.

What the hell was the bear doing here? Was this fucker stalking him? He saw a small-caliber rifle lying in the grass at the bear's feet and his muddled thoughts made a fuzzy connection. Had the bastard shot their tire out? He tried turning to look at the front wheel but another wave of nausea buckled his knees. He caught himself on the side of the truck and steadied himself.

"Go back to your boss," the bear growled. "Tell him no one else comes north."

"What? What the fuck are you talking about?"

The bear took a step forward and glared down at him. He seemed taller and much larger than Vern remembered.

"Pierce. Your boss. Tell him if he sends anyone else north, they won't come back. If he brings his trucks to Belle Plaine, I'll kill him. Understand?"

Vern's head was finally beginning to clear. He took a deep breath and tried to compose himself.

"You think I have any kind of authority there? I'm on a fucking scouting run. I'm low man on the totem. No one's going to listen to me."

The bear took a step back, reached under his coat, and brought out a huge goddamn revolver.

Jesus, Vern thought. *That's a forty-four magnum.*

The bear cocked the pistol as he raised it and Vern was suddenly, absolutely sure he was about to die. The bear held the pistol just inches from the center of his forehead for a second, then shifted his aim lower and to Vern's right.

The gun boomed and Vern jumped. After a second or two, realizing he was still alive, he turned and saw Baker lying half-way out of the truck, face-down on the ground. There was a pistol in his hand and a fist-sized hole in his head above his left ear.

He turned back to the bear, his ears ringing even worse than before.

"Deliver the message," the bear said, re-holstering his pistol. He sounded far away, like a distant god delivering judgement. "It's the only reason I don't kill you right now. And if I ever see you again, I *will* finish this."

The bear picked up his rifle, turned, and walked back up to the highway.

When he was gone, Vern dropped to his hands and knees, shaking uncontrollably and vomiting what little was left in his stomach onto the ground.

***

Erik sat in a small clump of trees just down the highway and watched the raider through his binoculars. After the man had finished puking a second time, he'd gotten to his feet and retrieved his cowboy hat from inside the wrecked truck. He'd then searched around for his pistol. Unable to find where Erik had thrown it, he'd returned and taken the pistol from the man Erik had shot. Then, after just standing there and looking around for a few minutes, he'd finally made his way up to the highway and started walking south.

As the man disappeared down the highway, Erik set the binoculars down and considered what he'd just done. He'd laid some pretty heavy threats down for the man to deliver. He doubted Pierce would be deterred. Just the opposite. If Pierce was even half the megalomaniac McClain had described, he'd throw his entire militia at Belle Plaine. But mobilizing all his men, weapons, and vehicles for an invasion would take time, and that would give Erik at least an additional day or two to convince Kate and her people to either prepare a defense or get the hell out of town.

Of course, if the raider had any real sense, he wouldn't return to Mankato at all. His boss wasn't going to be pleased with him or the message he had to deliver. He'd be smart to just keep heading south and disappear, forgetting he'd ever heard of Mankato or Captain Pierce.

Erik doubted the man had that much sense.

He took a deep breath and let it out slowly, glancing up at the sky. One thing always led to another and then another. If he had shown up at Dean's on any other day, the kid never would have followed him to his camp and he wouldn't have known about any of this. All of this would probably still be happening, but at least he wouldn't be a part of it. He'd be somewhere in the Dakotas by now, blissfully unaware and uninvolved in any of this shit.

The woods are lovely, dark and deep. But I have promises to keep, and miles to go before I sleep.

The words Ashley had quoted to him all those years ago at the mansion came back to him now. He could even hear her voice. He couldn't remember who she'd been quoting but he'd never forgotten the words. They summed up his life, then and now.

With another heavy sigh, he picked up his staff, stood, and resumed heading north, traveling through the trees just off the side of the highway.

Once again, he had a promise to keep. And once more, he had miles to go before he could sleep.

MAY 20

McClain's stomach felt as though he'd just swallowed a block of cold lead.

Shit, he thought. *This is not good.*

Standing at his door were Orlando and Vlad, the two biggest bad asses in Pierce's militia. And they looked grim.

"The captain wants to see you," Orlando said.

Not good at all.

McClain went to take his gun and belt off the peg on the wall but Vlad blocked his reach with his battle ax. "You won't be needing those," he said, grinning malevolently.

McClain gave a slight shrug, hoping it made him look unconcerned.

"Okay. Let's go see what the good captain wants."

He joined them outside where Orlando took up a position ahead of him and Vlad stayed a couple of steps behind. They walked in silence across the campus to Pierce's house. McClain noted the sky was getting a little dark to the northwest. There would probably be rain tonight. Good. He loved lying in bed at night listening to the rain.

Vlad and Orlando escorted him to Pierce's study. Jules was standing outside the closed door in his usual stance, arms folded and legs apart.

"Captain wants you two to wait out here until he needs you," Jules said to Orlando and Vlad in his deep, smooth voice.

The two men glanced at each other and then went to sit on the couch across the hallway.

Jules looked down at McClain. "I have to frisk you."

If there had been any question about it before, there was none now. He was in deep shit. He had never been frisked before any meeting with Pierce. In fact, he couldn't remember ever meeting with Pierce where he had not been carrying his fully loaded forty-five on his hip. He lifted his arms up and Jules patted his arms, down his sides, and down each leg.

As Jules was straightening back up, McClain thought he heard him say in a low voice, "He knows."

McClain met his eyes but saw nothing indicating Jules was trying to tell him anything. Maybe he'd just imagined it.

Jules opened the door and followed McClain in. Pierce was seated at his desk, pretending to read a book. McClain had never seen him with a book in his hand before and seriously doubted the idiot could even read. A decanter of whiskey and two glass tumblers sat on the desk. Vern was sitting in a chair next to the desk, holding his battered cowboy hat between his knees and looking like twelve miles of bad road.

McClain remembered that Vern and the two men he'd come to Mankato with had been sent on the scouting run to Belle Plaine. That was three days ago. He shouldn't be back yet. And where were the other two men? What the hell was going on?

Jules showed him to a chair opposite the desk and waited until McClain sat before stepping off to the side and resuming his characteristic stance.

Pierce waited a full minute before setting the book down and acknowledging McClain's presence with a single nod. He poured two fingers of whiskey into each tumbler, picked one up for himself, and indicated McClain should take the other.

"It's not the good shit you have squirreled away," Pierce said, "but not all of us have your connections."

McClain took the tumbler, noting that Vern wasn't holding one, and took a sip. His mouth was too dry to taste anything. Pierce's comment about "connections" worried him more than being frisked.

"So how are things going with the civilians?" Pierce asked lightly. "Are they getting enough to eat? Any discontented rumblings? Anything I should be aware of?"

McClain shook his head. "Nothing I've heard of. We've had a couple of problems with the generators and there's some discussion about the sewer situation but I think I've got those well in hand."

Pierce nodded. "Good. Good." He took a sip of whiskey. "How's that kid working out? You know, the one that came in a couple of weeks ago with the broken arm? Is he pulling his weight?"

McClain had to think about it before he remembered who Pierce was talking about. Only half his thoughts were on what Pierce was asking. The other half were still on why he was here to begin with.

"Willy. Yes, he's working out fine. Got him working at the water treatment facility, doing odd jobs and such until he can use his other arm."

Pierce drained the whiskey in his glass and then leaned back in his chair. He stared at McClain as though trying to read his thoughts, mindlessly drumming his fingers against his empty glass.

Here it comes.

"A couple days ago," Pierce said, "two of our guards walking the perimeter were found unconscious. They'd been hit in the head so hard that only one of them could remember anything. Bits and pieces is all. He said he remembered a big man wearing a fur coat and carrying a really big stick. Everything else was blank. That description ring any bells?"

"Sounds like the same man Vern and his men described," McClain said, glancing at Vern and then back to Pierce. "The same man who attacked Parsons and his men in Jordan. The one they call the bear."

Pierce nodded thoughtfully, pouring himself another tumbler of whiskey. He ignored Vern as though he wasn't even there.

"This bear. He seems hell bent on busting my balls lately. How much do you know about him?"

"Only what I've heard." He didn't like where this was going.

"So, you've never met the man. You have no idea who he is or why he seems to have taken an interest in our little community here." He stated these as facts.

"It's probably because of the Jordan raid," McClain offered. "It sounds like he's a little fond of the people there. When you sent your raiders in, maybe that pissed this bear off."

Pierce nodded. "Could be. But what I don't understand is why he would show up here, knock two of our guards out, and then leave without doing anything else. If he was trying to send us a message of some sort, it was a colossal failure."

Kind of like your raids on St. Peter and Jordan, McClain thought but didn't say anything.

"What I think," Pierce continued, "is that he came here to meet with someone. The guards just stumbled upon him and he had to take them out. Why he didn't outright kill them is anybody's guess."

"I thought he was a loner," McClain said. The whiskey was turning sour in his stomach. "Who would he have been here to meet?"

Jules' words came back to him: *He knows.*

Pierce ignored the question. He turned to Vern and abruptly changed the subject.

"So how did the scouting mission go?"

"We never got there," Vern said. "The bear ambushed us on the road. He shot out our tire. The truck rolled and Cody was killed in the crash. He shot Baker in the head."

Pierce's easy expression didn't change but his eyes flicked quickly to McClain and then back to Vern. McClain guessed Vern already told him all of this.

"Why didn't he kill you?" Pierce asked.

"He wanted me to bring a message back. He said you're not to go north. He said if you send anyone else north, they won't return. And if you go to Belle Plaine, he'll kill you."

Shit, McClain thought. Erik was just supposed to warn Belle Plaine, not challenge Pierce to a fight. Jesus, what had he started?

Pierce's gaze flicked between Vern and McClain a couple more times. Finally, to Vern he said, "Thank you. That will be all. Go get yourself cleaned up and get some rest."

He turned to Jules and nodded once. Jules followed Vern out of the room. Once they were gone, Pierce leaned back in his chair and turned to McClain again.

"Seems this bear knew all about our scouting party and our plans for Belle Plaine. My guess is someone tipped him off." His eyes were fixed evenly on McClain. "Just like how someone got word to St. Peter as to where and when we were coming."

He remained silent. As Jules warned him – and he was sure now Jules really did say it – Pierce knew everything. He was just toying with McClain, relishing the suspense of finally revealing him to be the traitor he was.

Fuck you, McClain thought. He would never give this bastard the satisfaction of a confession.

Jules returned. With him were Sara, Orlando, and Vlad. As Jules took up his usual position next to Pierce again, Sara sat in the chair recently vacated by Vern, not once looking at McClain. Orlando and Vlad took up positions just behind and on either side of him.

The sick feeling in his gut was suddenly much worse. Sara – she'd claimed she was visiting a friend the night Erik showed up at his place. Now he was sure she had been lying. She'd been in the house all along. She probably heard everything said between him and Erik.

God damn it. How could he have been so stupid? He'd been set up. That's why he'd been summoned to the post-raid meeting after Jordan. That's why Pierce asked him about Belle Plaine and so casually outlined his plans. It was bait for a suspected rat and he had eaten it up.

Corporal McClain wondered again if it would rain tonight. Ever since he was a boy, he'd always loved the comfortable, soothing sound of rain on the roof while he lay in his bed in the dark.

He knew now he would never hear that sound again.

MAY 21

Sitting behind a clump of bushes just off the highway a quarter mile southwest of Belle Plaine, Erik slowly worked the binoculars from left to right and then back again, watching the people of the town go about their daily business. There were several small fields and animal pens between him and the town. The fields hadn't been planted yet but there were a few people out there with shovels and hoes turning the soil. Another two or three were tending to the livestock, bringing armloads of hay to the cattle, grain to the horses, and buckets of scraps to the pigs. There were about twenty or thirty chickens wandering around freely. Just off the edge of the fields, three men and one woman appeared to be making routine repairs to one of the three greenhouses.

To the right was a large farmhouse with barns, out-buildings, and grain silos. An eighteen-wheeler and two pickup trucks sat in the driveway. Their tires were flat and they were covered with twenty-years' worth of dirt, debris, and rust. They hadn't moved since the storm. Unlike Mankato, these people were focused on food and self-sufficiency rather than technology and weapons.

A half-mile farther to the northeast was the edge of the town proper. Erik could see a cluster of houses and what looked like an old town hall or municipal building. People were moving among the houses and occasionally going into or out of the common building.

What McClain had told him was true. This was a nice, peaceful community of a couple hundred people. They were working together and making it work. This was the kind of place Mankato should be and what Jordan might someday become. The only thing he didn't see was any sort of defense. The place was wide open. He didn't see a single person carrying any kind of firearm. Hell, outside of a few pens for the animals, there was no fence, barrier, or defensible perimeter of any kind around the town.

He lowered the binoculars and leaned back against the tree. Taking a strip of deer jerky from his pocket, he chewed on it as he considered the best approach to take. He figured maybe he should wait until evening and then stroll right into that town hall or whatever it was. It might give them a scare but at least he would have their attention.

After a while, his thoughts drifted to the fact that Elk River was only a day or two north of here, and what McClain had told him about Ashley taking up with some guy called Thor. He was surprised he actually felt good about that. He had known her passion for a single night but he had never deluded himself into thinking she'd made love to him for any reason other than he was leaving the next day and she never expected to see him again. That was just the way it was. Besides, even if he had gone back, he doubted she would ever leave someone described as a Norse god for an unshaved, unwashed, belligerent bastard in a smelly old bear skin coat, such as himself.

Good for her, he thought, picturing how she'd looked that night in the flickering light of the lantern. He had no intention of going to Elk River and looking her up. He preferred to remember her as she was and to imagine that she'd finally found the hero she'd mistaken him for. If she was happy, then he was happy for her.

Taking another piece of jerky from his pocket, he chewed on it as he watched the people of Belle Plaine go about their work and daily lives, blissfully unaware of what would soon be heading their way. When evening finally drew close, he would go down and give them the bad news. Then he would head west and follow the river upstream into the forest, renewing his determination to never again get involved with the remains of civilization.

***

The common building he'd assumed was some sort of town hall because of all the activity turned out to be something far more obvious – a saloon. It had a long bar along one wall with glasses, mugs, and several dozen unlabeled bottles of alcohol sitting on the shelves behind it. Four large beer kegs also sat behind the bar with pump-siphons fitted to the tops.

There were three pool tables in the center of the room surrounded by eight round tables with chairs. Several of the tables were occupied by about a dozen men and half as many women talking, drinking, and playing cards or dominos when Erik walked in. There was a piano in the corner and, by God, there was actually someone playing it. Lanterns were set on each table and several more hung from the ceiling. An enormous fireplace that appeared to be a recent addition to the back wall held a crackling fire, keeping the room at a comfortable temperature.

The chatter and laughter at the tables abruptly died when he stepped through the door. The man playing the piano slowed his rhythm and hit a couple of wrong notes but quickly recovered.

He paused just inside the doorway to look around and let everyone see him. He then made his way to an empty table next to the bar. He leaned his staff against the table and took his coat off, laying it over one of the chairs before sitting down in another. He was fully aware of the stares and whispers his appearance was causing. Good. His entrance was having the desired effect.

One of the men at a nearby table stood and moved in his direction. He was a tall, gangly man with a narrow face and a chin full of white stubble. Erik was expecting him to stop at his table and begin with the questions, but the man continued past him and went around behind the bar. He filled a large, ceramic mug with beer from one of the kegs and then came back around and set it on the table in front of Erik.

"Welcome to Belle Plaine," the man said. "Name's Carl. I'm kind of the bartender here tonight."

He glanced at one of the empty chairs and then back to Erik. When Erik nodded, he took a seat.

"You just passing through or are you looking for someplace to hang your hat?" Carl asked.

Erik was unprepared for the man's friendly manner. He couldn't remember the last time someone had treated him as just a normal person and not some strange, possibly demonic figure that had crawled out of the woods to eat the town's children. It was an unfamiliar experience.

"I don't have a hat," he said. "I'm looking for someone called Kate or whoever is in charge around here. I've got some news she's not going to like but needs to hear."

"Kate...?" The man rubbed his stubbly chin. Behind him, the noise and chatter picked up again as the saloon patrons decided Erik wasn't going to go on a rampage and kill them all.

The piano player made a smooth transition to another tune. Erik recognized it – *Somewhere in the Night*. It brought back a memory of him and Tyler camped along a creek, half-drunk on peach brandy and talking about girls.

"You mean Belle?" the man asked.

"Whoever's in charge," Erik repeated, remembering McClain had told him Kate was sometimes called Belle. "It's important."

"Gotchya," Carl the bartender said. He stood and went back to his table. He had a brief, hushed conversation with another, younger man. The younger man stood, shot a curious glance toward Erik, and then quickly left the saloon. Carl the gangly bartender sat back down at his own table and rejoined the conversation he'd left.

Erik lifted the mug of beer and took a drink. It was warm but surprisingly good. He took a longer swallow and then sat back to wait for the arrival of whoever the younger man had gone out to fetch. The others in the bar stole occasional glances his way but they seemed surprisingly at ease with strangers.

Half-way through his beer, Erik glanced to the door as three noisy, boisterous young men entered. Two were probably in their mid-twenties while the tall one in the center appeared to be a bit younger, maybe not even twenty years old yet. This younger one had a strong, handsome face, longish brown hair, and green eyes. Despite his age, he appeared to be the leader of the trio. He was the youngest person Erik had seen in a long time, even younger than the raider whose arm he'd broken.

The three were talking and laughing loudly. The tall kid in the center took a bulky cloth sack from over his shoulder and dropped it onto the first table they came to.

"How'd the hunt go, Chris?" one of the men at a table near the fireplace called out.

"What's the count now?" another asked.

The tall kid, apparently named Chris, reached into the sack. "Five thousand," he replied. He pulled a flat, white, rectangular object from the bag and held it high in the air. "Five thousand and *one*," he shouted.

The entire room broke out in cheering and applause as Chris turned in a circle, smiling, taking bows, and holding the object high so all could see it. His two buddies were also cheering and taking bows.

It took Erik a few seconds to recognize the object as an old cell phone. The bag must have been full of them.

He took another drink of beer, wondering what in hell someone could possibly use an old cell phone for, much less five thousand of them. Whatever they had in mind, this kid and his friends must have been collecting them for a long time.

As the cheering died, the kid, Chris, finally noticed Erik sitting at the table by the bar. He dropped the cell phone back into the bag and directed his friends' attentions to Erik.

"Whoa-ho-ho," Chris said, he and his friends moving in Erik's direction. "What in the hell do we have here?"

"Leave him alone, Chris," Carl the bartender called from his table. "He's just passing through. Let him drink his beer in peace."

Chris waved the bartender off and directed his friends to either side of Erik's table. Erik leaned back in his chair, regarding the boys as he would three tree squirrels who thought they were pretty darn tough.

Chris put his hands on the table and leaned forward, looking Erik up and down. "Jesus H Christ. What cave did you crawl out of, old man?"

One of his friends picked up Erik's coat. "Look at this. Is this bearskin?" He dropped it back onto the chair, shook his hand, and made a disgusted face. "Phew! Smells like it was dead a while before you skinned it."

"Naw, that's just him," the third one said. "These mountain men don't take baths. They use their stink to keep the wolves away."

"Boys…," Carl called again. "I'd advise you to leave that man alone. I don't think he wants to be bothered."

"Well maybe he's bothering us," Chris called back over his shoulder.

"Hey," the first one said, glancing at Erik's coat again. "You don't suppose this is *the bear*, do you?"

"Bear, my ass," Chris said.

"How about it, old man?" the second one said. "Did you kill a bear with your bare hands and skin it alive?"

"How in hell could he skin it alive if he just killed it?" the first one sneered.

"Shut up," Chris ordered. He leaned in closer to Erik. "How about it, old man? Are you the bear? Do you shit in the woods?"

This elicited riotous laughter from both of his friends.

Erik calmly went to pick up his mug to take another drink. Chris's hand shot out and pinned his arm to the table. The kid was fast and surprisingly strong.

"Not so fast, old man." Chris nodded to the mug of beer. "How are you going to pay for that? You don't think you can just come in here and drink for free, do you?"

"Chris, goddammit!" Carl hollered, a note of urgency in his tone.

Erik used his other hand to reach into his shirt pocket. Keeping his eyes on Chris, he pulled out one of the gold coins he'd saved from the raiders and tossed it onto the table.

Chris's eyes went to the coin. He frowned. "What the fuck is that?"

With a sudden, swift movement, Erik swiped both of Chris's arms out from under him. Chris fell forward. Erik caught his head and slammed it down hard onto the table. Standing in a single, swift move, he dumped Chris, coin, and beer onto the floor, flipping the table on top of the kid. Both of his friends jumped back.

He stepped onto the table and then over it, bringing himself directly in front of one of the other two. The kid drew his arm back, preparing to throw a punch. Erik grabbed him by the front of his shirt and threw him back against the bar. The edge of the bar caught the kid low in the ribs, knocking the wind out of his lungs. The kid groaned and fell to the floor.

He turned to the second, who was backpedaling away with his hands out in front of himself.

"Hey, man. We didn't want no trouble."

Erik stepped on and over the table again, advancing on the kid a couple of steps. He stopped and turned at the sound of Chris throwing the table off himself and getting to his feet. Instead of standing straight up, Chris launched himself forward, catching Erik at the waist with his shoulder, lifting him off his feet, and driving him backwards.

Erik crashed back into the second man and they all went back over another table and down to the floor with Chris on top. The kid's speed caught Erik by surprise. Chris was swinging punches at him but he was too close to land them effectively. Erik headbutted him in the cheekbone below his left eye, stunning him. He pushed Chris roughly off to the side and was rolling over to get to his feet when he felt a hand grab the back of his shirt and jerk him off the floor.

"That'll be enough of that," a commanding voice said.

The man set him on his feet but kept an iron grip on the back of his shirt, forcing Erik to face the bar. He tried to turn but the man was stronger than a bull moose. He was tall – almost six inches taller than Erik – with a square, clean-shaven jaw, longish blonde hair, and blue eyes.

Without releasing his grip on Erik's shirt, the man reached down with his other hand and caught Chris by his own collar as he was struggling to get up. The blond man hauled the kid the rest of the way to his feet.

"Time for you to go, Chris," the blonde giant said. "And take your friends with you." He let go of Chris's shirt and pointed to the door.

Chris, his face flushed and his cheek already starting to swell, glared at Erik briefly and then motioned for his two friends to follow him. As they were heading to the door, the blonde man turned to Erik.

"If I let you go, are you going to behave?"

"They started it," Erik said, pointing after the departing boys.

The man studied him, looking Erik up and down, and then let out a bellowing laugh. He released his grip on Erik's shirt.

"I'm sure they did," he said, thumping Erik on the back. "Come with me. I'll take you to see Belle."

***

"Sorry about that ruckus back there," the blonde man said as he walked beside Erik, leading him toward the large farmhouse on the west side of town Erik had seen earlier. "Chris and his friends can get a bit rambunctious sometimes but they're mostly good kids, hard workers. I'm Eben, by the way." He held out his hand.

Erik shook the big man's hand, noting it completely engulfed his own. "Erik."

"Erik," Eben repeated and mulled the name over. "Jason, the man who came and got me, seemed to think you might be the one they call the bear."

"That name does tend to follow me around."

"Where are you coming from, Erik the bear?"

"South of here. Mankato. I just need to speak with this Belle person of yours and then I'll be on my way."

"Where are you from originally?" Eben asked, ignoring the subject of Mankato and why Erik was here. "I mean, before the storm."

Erik was surprised at his use of the term "storm" to describe the event that changed the world forever. Most everyone besides himself called it "the end" or "doomsday" or "the apocalypse."

"Iowa," he answered.

Eben nodded. "Ever been up this way before?"

"All the time, hunting and fishing. I usually keep to the woods west of here. I don't hang around people much. Don't think I've ever been through this town."

"Ever been through any of the other towns around here? Minneapolis? Elk River? St. Paul? We trade with a lot of them."

"Not recently. Been through Elk River and a lot of towns north and south of here along the highway, but that was a long time ago."

They walked in silence for a while, approaching the farm. Finally, Eben asked, "So how do you know Belle? You asked for her by name."

"I don't know her. I was told I needed to get a message to whoever was in charge up here. The man who sent me said her name was Kate but that everyone calls her Belle. He said she was an older woman and wasn't sure if she'd still be alive."

"Oh Belle's alive alright," Eben said. They reached the house and Eben held the door open for him. "She won't be back until tomorrow. You can spend the night here if you want. This is her house."

Erik stopped. "I don't want to sleep in someone else's house when they're not here."

Eben chuckled. "It's my house too. It's a big place. We share it. Don't worry. You'll be in the guest room."

Erik accepted his invitation and Eben showed him into the house, surprising him by turning the lights on.

"Yes," Eben said, seeing his reaction, "we're not all primitive around here. We do have a few working generators but we use them sparingly."

Eben gave him a brief tour. It was a large, two-story house with five bedrooms, three baths, and a kitchen designed for feeding a small army. After the tour, Eben showed him to a bedroom with its own bathroom off to the side.

"Make yourself at home. I'll go make us a bite to eat." He opened the door to the bathroom and turned the lights on. "Feel free to take a bath before dinner. We've got plenty of hot water and soap. And you'll find a pair of scissors and a razor in the cabinet there if you want to clean up that beard of yours. Not that it doesn't suit you but it looks like you've been trimming it with a knife."

Erik glanced in the mirror above the sink and ran his hand over his beard. He hadn't seen his own reflection in a long time. Damn! No wonder people tended to avoid him.

"Yeah, I suppose I could do with a bit of a clean-up," he admitted, glancing around the bathroom. He figured he was going to have to take full advantage of this. He wasn't going to shave his beard but he'd take Eben's advice and trim it up a bit with the scissors.

"I'll leave you to it then. Come on down to the kitchen when you're ready."

After Eben left, Erik turned the water in the bathtub to full hot and stripped down, anticipating the luxury of his first hot bath in twenty years.

MAY 22

Vern awoke to the absolute certainty he was about to die.

It was early in the morning, well before sunup, and a hulking form was looming over his bed. His immediate thought was the bear had somehow tracked him down and was now about to either break his neck or ram that big damn knife of his deep into his chest. The first would be quick. The second would hurt like hell. He hoped it would be the first.

The looming shape spoke.

"Get up. You need to leave here. Now."

The voice was deep and mellow. It was Jules.

Vern quickly sat up with his back to the headboard of the bed. What in the hell was Jules doing in the bunkhouse?

"Wha... what?" he stammered. "Why?"

"The captain is going to have you killed."

"Shit." Wide awake now, he threw the covers off to the side and slid off the bed. "Why? What'd I do?" He had no idea why Pierce would want him dead. But if Jules was saying it, it must be true.

He started rummaging for his clothes on the floor. The starlight coming through the window didn't provide much light and he had to feel around. Jules must have eyes like a cat to move as quietly as he did in the dark. He finally found his pants and began pulling them on.

"He thinks you're working with the bear."

Vern stopped, his pants up but unfastened.

"What? Why the hell would he think that?"

"Because you've met him twice and you're still alive."

Vern hesitated. "How's that my fault? He killed my men."

"Exactly," Jules said. "You came back from that scouting mission alone."

Vern finished fastening his pants and began feeling for his shirt. "Only because he wanted me to deliver a message. Is Pierce fucking paranoid?"

"Yes. He's already had McClain and Parsons killed. He's cleaning house."

"Jesus Christ." Vern slipped his shirt on and began buttoning it. He didn't care why Pierce would have had McClain or Parsons killed. It was his own ass he was worried about.

"Fuck. Both times I've met that sonofabitch, I thought for sure he was going to kill me. He killed Cody by wrecking our truck and then he shot Baker in the head. Why in hell would I be working with him?" A thought struck him and he stopped and looked at the hulking shape in front of him. "What about Willy? Does Pierce think he's also involved in this grand conspiracy?"

Jules hesitated before replying, "Not anymore."

It took Vern a second or two to realize what he meant. "Ah, shit. God damn it." The kid was a screwup but he didn't deserve to be murdered because of some asshole's paranoid delusions. He should never have set foot in this fucked-up town.

He finished buttoning his shirt and then strapped on his gun belt and found his boots, coat, and hat. He turned to Jules again.

"Why are you telling me this, warning me?"

When Jules didn't say anything, Vern felt a sense of dread.

"Oh shit. He sent you, didn't he? You're supposed to let me get a little ways out of town and then kill me as a deserter."

"No."

"Then why?"

Jules paused again. "I don't know."

Vern stared at him. It was impossible to see the big man's face in the darkness of the room. Jules could have killed him in his sleep and then dressed him and dropped his body anywhere on the road if Pierce wanted it to look like he'd been killed in the act of desertion. But Jules hadn't killed him. Jules didn't even wear a gun. Was the big man warning him despite Pierce? Maybe there was some dissension in the upper ranks.

"Why don't you kill him?" Vern asked. "You're alone with Pierce more than anyone. Why not just kill him? You could take over or put someone else in charge."

"That's not for me to decide."

"Then who?"

Another pause. "Maybe the bear."

His answer took Vern by surprise. The bear? What the hell? Did Jules think the bear had been sent by some higher power? Did he think the arrival of the bear somehow heralded Pierce's eventual downfall?

"I don't know, man," Vern said, shaking his head as he pulled on his boots. "I think we've probably seen the last of the bear. I don't think he's coming back this way."

Jules didn't say anything.

Vern finished getting his clothes and gear together. He glanced around the dark room even though he couldn't see anything but vague shapes. He didn't own anything other than what he was wearing right now. Looking to Jules again, he asked, "Which way should I go?"

"West."

Yeah, that made sense. Pierce's militia controlled most of the towns east and north of here. There weren't any towns of any size to the west or south. And if Pierce sent someone after him, he'd probably assume Vern had headed south.

"Okay," Vern said. He held his hand out. "Thanks."

Jules ignored his hand. "Thank me by never coming back. If you do, I'll have to assume you'll tell the captain I was here tonight."

"I won't."

"I've never had to kill anyone before."

Vern felt his mouth go dry. He swallowed hard. This was the second man in as many days who threatened to kill him if they ever saw him again. He decided if there ever was a time to get the hell out of Dodge and never look back, it was right fucking now.

Without another word, he turned and left the room, deciding to put Mankato behind him and never look back.

***

It had been snowing for almost eight days now. Sometimes it came down so heavy he couldn't see the trees outside the window. Other times it was light, but then the wind would blow and the trees would disappear again in all that swirling, driving whiteness.

There was no wind this morning so the snow was falling straight down. As Erik stood at the window, he thought of how it just kept coming and coming. How could there be that much snow in the clouds? It was already two feet deep. Some of the drifts from yesterday's wind were eight or ten feet high. In a couple of days, three at the most, he would have to venture out for supplies. Maybe he should go now, before the wind started blowing again. But if he got caught out there, if the wind suddenly kicked up again, it would be death for both of them.

He turned from the window and went back to join April on the couch in front of the fireplace. She was wrapped to her chin in several layers of blankets. The only parts of her that were visible were her nose, her eyes, and a bit of her long, dark hair. They had spent the last two months making their way slowly up Interstate 35 from Iowa. They had finally been forced to stop at a farmhouse a few miles outside of a small town in southern Minnesota because of the worsening weather. It was only mid-September, but winter was here now and it was bad.

April opened her cocoon of blankets just enough to allow Erik to slide in next to her. He put his arm around her small shoulders and she snuggled up against him for additional warmth.

"Are you still cold?" Erik asked, hugging her close. He had added more wood to the fire a few minutes ago and felt the room was too warm now. April had been chilled since last night. Though she felt warm to Erik, he could feel her shivering beneath the blankets.

"I'm warmer now." Her voice was muffled because she had her face buried in the blankets against Erik's chest. He heard her cough softly.

"Are you hungry?"

"Not yet."

She squirmed under the blankets to get more comfortable and her hair tickled Erik's nose.

He opened his eyes and blinked rapidly, feeling a little disoriented. He was in a bed, in a house. He was covered in heavy, warm blankets and his head was on a pillow. There was morning light slanting in through the windows.

Ashley was lying on her side on top of the covers next to him. She had her head propped up with her hand. She was twenty years older. It showed in the small creases at the corners of her eyes. Her face was fuller and her dark hair was much longer, but he could never forget those feline green eyes and that enigmatic smile.

"Good morning, hero." She leaned over and kissed him lightly on the nose.

Erik was too stunned to reply. He stared at her, wondering where she had come from. Or was this just another dream?

Her fingers stroked his newly trimmed beard. "You've grown fuzzy."

"Ashley." It came out as a whisper. He still wasn't sure if this was real or a dream.

It couldn't be real.

She put her arm over his chest and laid her head on his shoulder.

"Oh my god, I can't believe how much I missed you." She hugged him through the covers. Her voice was muffled by the blankets, just like April's was in his dream. "I couldn't believe it when Eben said you were here."

Erik worked his arms out from under the blankets and wrapped them around her. This was real. She was real. But how? He held her tight and breathed in the scent of her hair. All his memories from the mansion at Elk River came rushing back to him. It had been so long ago, so many miles and years between then and now. But it felt like only yesterday.

"I missed you too," he said.

She raised her head and placed her chin on his chest, looking up at him with a slight smile on her lips.

"So, where have you been, mister? You don't call, you don't write, and then suddenly you show up out of the blue to crash in my guest bedroom after you start a fight in our tavern. Seriously? A bar fight?"

"I didn't start that fight," he protested.

"And then you tell Eben you have to talk to the old hag in charge around here."

"I don't think I used the term 'old hag' but, yeah, I have to talk to whoever's in charge. I was told it was someone named Kate."

"Kate died two years ago."

Erik was confused. "That man – Eben? – he said she was still alive. I guess everyone calls her Belle?"

Ashley kept staring at him, that slight smile still on her lips. Finally, she hugged him again and said, "I remember you being more intuitive than this. I think you've been stomping around the woods a little too long. Not enough contact with people."

"What do you mean?"

She sat up. "*I'm* Belle, you goofy mountain man, as in 'the belle of Belle Plaine.' It's kind of an honorary title, really. Kate was the belle before me. When she died, I sort of inherited the name."

"You're Belle?" he asked, more than a little surprised. "You're in charge around here?"

"Well, me and Eben. We're kind of a team. And Chris. You know, the one you got into a fight with last night?"

Erik pictured the tall, incredibly strong Nordic man who'd lifted him by his shirt. Ashley was right. Not being around people for so long was making him a little slow on the uptake.

"Eben. He was with you up at the mansion?"

"Yes. He's been such a big help all these years."

"McClain said people called him Thor."

She laughed. "Oh yeah, a lot of people called him that up there. I guess he does look like some kind of Viking god." And then she frowned. "McClain? *Corporal* McClain? When did you see him?"

"A few days ago. He's the one who sent me up here. He's in Mankato.

I guess he came through Belle Plaine a long time ago, back when Kate was running things."

"I always wondered where he ended up," she said. "I always had the impression he was jealous of Eben and that's why he left."

"He was, in a way, but he left for a variety of reasons."

She laid her head back down on his chest and sighed.

"So… you and Eben are…?" He let the question trail off. He wasn't sure he if really wanted to know the answer or not. But he was damned sure he didn't want that blonde giant walking in here to find him lying in bed next to his woman. That would not be good. That would be a really bad day.

Ashley lifted her head again and gave him the same mischievous look he remembered from that night they'd first spoken on the balcony at the mansion.

"Oh my god, Erik. Are you jealous?"

"I'm just… no… I was just wondering…"

She laughed. "You don't have to be. Eben and I are just good friends. He's the big brother I never had."

He felt a rush of relief. Not only did it mean he wouldn't have to worry about Eben breaking him in two, but also that maybe Ashley was still single and unattached. It was odd and he didn't know why he should feel that way. It wasn't like he'd come up here expecting them to suddenly rush into each other's arms and fall madly in love. Hell, he hadn't even known she was here, and they hadn't seen each other for twenty years.

Ashley pulled the blankets down a bit and planted a couple of small kisses on his chest.

"And you don't have to worry about him being jealous of you, either." She kissed him again. "He's gay."

That caught Erik by surprise. "What? Really?"

"Hm um." She looked up at him. "So, are you glad to see me?"

He smiled back at her. "I am. Although…"

She raised her eyebrows. "Although?"

"Well, the last time I saw you, you said if we ever met again, we would discuss those weird dreams of mine. Like that one I had at the mansion the night before I left."

There was that subtle, beautiful smile again. "And…?"

"And, well, you know, I kind of liked that last weird dream. I was sort of hoping I'd have another."

She sat up and swung one leg over him, straddling him over the blankets. She began unbuttoning her shirt.

"Well then, I guess we're just going to have to *discuss* this, aren't we?"

***

Ashley lay in Erik's arms, sweaty and exhausted in a way she hadn't been in a very long time. She felt completely drained, breathless, and yet wonderfully content. The years and miles separating them had transformed the determined, passionate boy she'd found so intriguing back then into this strong, solidly built man lying beside her now, his passion and determination still evident in the tireless but caring way he made love.

She knew he hadn't come here looking for her. It was only a coincidence they'd run across one another again. He had left her and everyone else at the mansion twenty years ago to keep a promise and he had never returned. Whatever he'd done in all those missing years, wherever he'd been, it had changed him, hardened him in a lot of ways. She could feel that. She could see it in his eyes. Now, he was the man everyone called the bear. He had no roots and went wherever he pleased. It wouldn't surprise her if he went back to the woods today, tomorrow, or even the next day.

But for now, he could be hers once more.

Her fingers traced small circles on his chest while he rubbed her back with one hand and stroked her hair with the other. She felt the long, ragged scars on his upper left shoulder, extending down and across his chest. She'd seen them before but hadn't thought much about them. She'd been a little... distracted. Now she was curious. She pushed herself up and examined them. There were four large, red welts extending all the way down from his shoulder to half-way across his chest. They were thick and showed signs of the rough stitching that had closed them up.

"My God," she breathed. "What happened? What did this?"

Erik glanced down at his chest. "My namesake. He gave me those and I took his hide in return. I figure it was a fair trade."

"Jesus. You mean you really *were* attacked by a bear? And you killed it? That's not just a story?"

"Never store food in your camp," he said. "Bear smells food. Bear walks into camp looking for food. Bear sees you..." He shrugged. "Bear decides maybe you taste better."

"You killed it with your bare hands?"

He laughed. "That's a good story but not quite right. I tried to shoot it but that first bullet was a dud. The bear didn't give me a second chance. It knocked me down and did all this with one swipe. All I could do was grab my knife and ram it into its neck as deep as I could when it came in to finish me off. I must have hit an artery or something because the next thing I knew I was covered in blood and a few hundred pounds of dead bear."

She traced one of the scars with her finger.

"Who did the stitching?"

"An old guy I know in a little village south of here. Took me thirty, forty minutes to pull myself out from under that damn bear. When I finally got out, I skinned it and took the pelt to him. He stitched me up and then made me a coat from the hide. It's warm as hell. He's a good leather worker. Makes me all of my clothes."

"You took the time to skin the bear before getting help? Jesus, Erik. By the looks of these, you could have bled to death by then. You *should* have bled to death."

He gave a shrug. "I packed them with hot ashes from my campfire to cauterize the wounds and stop the bleeding. Anyway, I was a long way from help. Figured if I died along the way, I may as well have something warm to cover my bones."

"And that makes what kind of sense?"

She put her chin on his chest again and looked up at him.

"So, aside from killing bears and becoming a legend, what else have you been doing with your time?" She hesitated, not sure if she should ask or not, but then did anyway. "Did you and Tyler ever make it home? Did you find your sister?"

His smile faded a little and his gaze slid away from hers.

"Tyler didn't make it. We met some… I don't know, crazies, I guess. Tyler got shot. He saved both our lives that night. I thought he was okay but he died later after we started south again." There was a long pause and then he said, "I kept going. I finally got home but Sam was already gone. So was my mother. They'd been gone the whole time. I guess my dad survived the storm and he buried Sam and my mom in the backyard. He left a note saying he was going south."

"I'm sorry," she whispered. She remembered how he had talked about his little sister, how he would stop at nothing to keep his promise to go back for her. She didn't say anything for a while and then asked, "Why didn't you go south after your father?"

"I guess maybe because we were never really that close, and because I'd already been on my own for so long. I stayed for a couple of days before leaving. I didn't know where I wanted to go. I think I headed north because it was familiar. I came across a little girl – April. She was about Sam's age and she didn't have anyone. She was all alone. I thought I could bring her back up to the mansion. We only got about half-way before that first big winter hit."

"I remember that winter. It was really bad for us as well."

"We took shelter in a farmhouse just over the Minnesota border. I thought we would be okay but she got sick. Pneumonia, I think." He sighed, his eyes staring over her head. "She died a few days later. After that, I don't know. I guess I just gave up. I walked into the woods and I've lived there ever since."

They were both quiet for a while. Ashley thought she was beginning to understand him a little more now. He was haunted by all the people he'd lost – Seth, Tyler, Sam, his mother, April, and God knew how many others over the years. No wonder he lived in the woods and avoided people. He was running from their memories. Everyone she knew had lost someone, but Erik seemed somehow cursed to continue losing those he cared about the most. He was carrying so much pain and sadness, he was afraid to get close to anyone now. He wasn't taking the easy way out. He was just sparing himself any more pain and suffering.

"You could have come back," she said softly. "I guess I always hoped you would."

"I wanted to. But it seemed like everyone I cared about, everyone I tried to help... There were a few times I ran across smaller groups of survivors here and there, but it always seemed to end the same way, with someone's death, usually everyone but me." He paused. "After a while, I thought it would be better if I just stayed away from people entirely."

She laid her head back down and caressed his chest for a while as he resumed stroking her hair. A thought struck her and she asked, "So all this time since the mansion... You've never been with anyone else?"

Erik didn't say anything and when she looked up at him, she saw he was smiling.

"What's that shit-eating grin for?" she asked.

"You want to know if I've been saving myself for you?"

"No, I was just curious. It's been a long time. I wouldn't expect you to save yourself for anyone this long."

He leaned forward and kissed her on the lips. "It was worth the wait."

She was ready to let the subject drop and then realized he hadn't given her an answer.

"So, have you?"

"Well...," he said, grinning again and looking up at the ceiling, "I *was* saving myself, but there was this really cute wolf that came through my camp last month – beautiful eyes, thick, silky fur, and a tail to die for. She played hard to get and it was a hell of a chase but I finally ran her down. Man, she wasn't happy about that at all. But, you know, when the urge hits..."

She slapped him on the chest, laughing. "That's disgusting!"

The door to the bedroom opened a crack and Eben's head poked inside.

"Sorry," he said. "I heard voices and figured you were both up. Breakfast will be ready in a few. I'll keep it warm for you." His head disappeared again and the door closed.

"That reminds me," Erik said. "How did he know who I was? I mean, in relation to you. I figure he must have told you who I was, unless you awaken all your guests like this."

"He told me. I might have mentioned you once or twice over the years. He didn't know you were the one I'd told him about at first, but then after you told him your name and about how you'd been in Elk River a long time ago, and that you were from Iowa, he put it together that you were my long-lost hero."

Erik laughed. "That hero crap needs to stop. I'm just a guy who lives in the woods, kills bears, and screws wolves when the urge hits." He bent down and gave her another kiss. "Think we should get up and get some breakfast?"

"In a bit. He said he'll keep it warm. But right now, I'm hungry for a little more of this." She reached under the blankets and gripped him firmly. He surprised her with his stamina. They'd just finished a rather vigorous round of love making but he was already growing hard again in her hand. It excited her and made her feel young and frisky, like she was nineteen years old again.

"We can do it wolf style. I'll even howl if you want me to."

He pulled her closer, giving an enthusiastic, "Woof!"

***

The smell of fresh-baked bread wafting through the house was driving Erik to ravenous hunger. He'd caught the first whiff as he'd been getting dressed. Now, entering the kitchen behind Ashley, he was ready to take on two or three bears if it meant getting a bite of that bread.

Eben was removing a steaming loaf from the oven as they walked in.

He turned his head at their entrance. The giant, blonde man who could lift him with one arm looked almost comical bending over the stove in red oven mitts and a white, flower-print apron.

"Good morning," he greeted them with a broad grin. "How'd the reunion go?" He set the hot bread on the stovetop.

Ashley, who barely came up to his chest, gave him a playful slap on the arm. "You... You didn't tell him who I was. You let him think Belle was some frumpy old lady."

"I didn't want to spoil the surprise," he said, still with a big grin on his face. He winked at Erik. "Some surprises are just too good to spoil, don't you think?"

"I do now," Erik admitted, glancing to Ashley. Underneath the aroma of the fresh-baked bread, he was smelling bacon and sausage as well. It was almost more than he could stand.

"I see you found the clothes I laid out for you," Eben said over his shoulder, bustling about the kitchen, getting things ready. "Don't worry about your animal skins. I didn't throw them out, though I suspect they could scamper away on their own if they wanted to. I hung them on a line outside to let the fresh air and sun work on them. I hope the neighbors don't complain."

Erik had wondered about that. After he and Ashley had gotten out of bed, he looked around for his coat and deer-hide clothes but found they had been replaced by a pile of neatly folded jeans, underwear, socks, and a heavy flannel shirt. It reminded him of his and Tyler's first day at the mansion, when Saundra spirited away their dirty, ragged clothes and replaced them with clean ones while they were in the showers.

He took a seat at the small kitchen table across from Ashley and stared in amazement as Eben laid out plates of sausage, bacon, scrambled eggs, hash-browns, butter, and the freshly sliced loaf of bread. There were also salt and pepper shakers and a pitcher of milk on the table with three tall glasses.

"This is... amazing," Erik said. "I haven't seen a breakfast like this since I was a kid."

"This is a farming community, after all," Ashley said. "We've worked hard on becoming self-sufficient for years. We've got fields, greenhouses, livestock... No more scrounging for canned goods and stale loaves of bread."

Eben joined them at the table. "All of this is thanks to our late benefactor, Kate. She was the one who really got this community going. If it wasn't for her, we'd probably be scattered to the four winds by now.

Like Ashley said, we'd still be scrounging for leftovers from the old world." He nodded to the food on the table. "Dig in. Help yourself. We've got plenty."

Erik loaded his plate with a large helping of everything.

"How did you come to be down here?" he asked as they began to eat. "This place is quite a ways south of Elk River."

Ashley explained how, after about eight years, the community in Elk River, still centered around the mansion, had grown to around twenty people. They tried some farming by digging up and planting the nearby golf course but it hadn't gone very well – no one in the community knew much about growing crops. It was while Eben was out on a supply run one day that he came across another survivor who told him about Belle Plaine. Eben, acting as emissary, made contact. By the next spring, almost the entire population around the mansion had moved to Belle Plaine.

"What happened to Saundra?" Erik asked. "McClain told me about Sergeant Ortiz but he didn't mention Saundra."

"She died a few years after McClain left," Ashley said, "before we moved down here. We think it was her heart or maybe a stroke. She woke up one morning feeling weak and disoriented. By the end of the day…" She trailed off and looked down at her plate.

Eben reached over and squeezed her hand. To Erik, he said, "Saundra was a mother to us all, especially to Ashley. Without her, we never would have become a community, a family."

"I remember," Erik said.

Eben continued, explaining how Kate, whom everyone called Belle, welcomed them in as she welcomed all survivors – as long as you were willing to work, you were welcome in Belle Plaine. As Saundra had done before, Kate took Ashley under her wing and became her teacher and mentor. The two women co-led the community while Eben continued his work as emissary to the surrounding, smaller communities and scattered groups of survivors. Within two years, Belle Plaine grew from a small farm to a mostly self-sufficient village of over eighty people.

"And Kate?" Erik asked. "Or Belle?"

"She passed away two years ago," Eben said. "She died as she lived – outdoors, working in the fields and taking care of the animals. After that, the people here naturally turned to Ashley as their leader, even giving her their highest compliment, the name of Belle."

"From what I can see," Erik said, "you two have done an amazing job following her legacy. I think she would be honored. And this food…

wow!" He had cleaned his plate so thoroughly it looked as though it had just been washed.

"I just wish it could last," Ashley sighed.

"What do you mean?" Erik asked, helping himself to another plateful of eggs, bacon, sausage, and bread.

"The winters," Eben said. "I'm sure you've noticed how they arrive earlier and last longer every year. The summers are getting so short the crops barely have time to mature."

"Kind of hard not to notice. I've been thinking it's part of some weather cycle that will eventually work itself out."

Eben shook his head. "Unfortunately, it doesn't look like it's going to work itself out. A man came through Elk River years ago, just before we moved down here. He came down from North Dakota, I believe. He said he'd been a climatologist at some university. According to him, we were already past the tipping point of climate change when that storm kicked it into high gear. It tipped the scales so much, now we're not only heading for a new ice age, but we're heading there at an unprecedented rate."

"Ice age?" Erik said. "Don't those take like thousands of years?"

"He was talking decades," Ashley said. "In fact, he said it had already started and it was accelerating exponentially every year."

"And from what we're seeing, it seems he was right," Eben added. "Other people have come down from north of here since then. They say most of Canada is completely frozen over year-round now and it's heading our way. That's why we're already making plans to move everyone in Belle Plaine farther south, maybe as far as Kansas or Colorado in the next couple of years. My brother has – had – a large ranch in Colorado called Nova Springs. It's plenty big enough for everyone here. Might be a good place to start over."

"Jesus," Erik said, thinking about all the people and animals, even the greenhouses. "That's going to take some serious planning and work."

"Moses did it," Eben said, "if you believe in your Bible stories. But instead of just marching everyone blindly across a desert and wandering aimlessly for forty years, we're looking at a more deliberate, staged migration – send small groups ahead first to prepare for the arrival of each successive group. Just kind of leap-frog south like that until we get to wherever it is we're going."

"If anyone can pull it off, Eben can," Ashley said. "We've discovered he's a genius when it comes to civil engineering and logistics. He's the one who moved us down here from the mansion without a single hiccup or problem."

Erik thought about it and admired their ambition. Between Ashley and Eben, this was a community with an eye on survival and growth over the long haul, completely opposite of what he'd seen in Mankato. He sat back in his chair and sighed. He was going to have to tell them.

"You remember last night when I said I had something important to tell you?"

Eben nodded.

"Does it have something to do with Mankato?" Ashley asked.

Erik was surprised. "How did you know that?"

She shrugged. "You told me you spoke with Corporal McClain down there. We know it's some kind of quasi-military community. We've had people come through here who've had dealings with them. We took in over a dozen people from St. Peter last week. Just stands to reason that's what you want to talk about."

"It is. But Mankato isn't quasi anything. It's a military dictatorship, pure and simple. The guy in charge down there calls himself Captain Pierce. McClain told me he has no real military background but that hasn't stopped him from building himself a pretty big militia. They're well-armed and organized. They've got military weapons and working vehicles, and they've put all the communities south of here down there under their boot."

"Sounds like they've raided some National Guard armories," Eben said. "I know there are a couple down in that area.

"That would explain the weapons and trucks," Erik said. "They have fifty-caliber machine guns mounted in the backs of a couple of the pickups I've seen. I don't know about explosives or what else they might have but they seem to have plenty of gasoline, guns, and ammo."

"And they're heading this way," Ashley guessed.

Erik nodded. "McClain said they'd be here within a week or two, maybe sooner. I stopped one of their scouting parties on my way up here but that's only going to buy you a couple of days. McClain was going to try and slow them down on his end. I don't know how much he can do, but nothing either of us do is going to stop them. They know you're up here. They've already scouted you once so they know you have resources and supplies. And they *are* coming."

Ashley looked at Eben. "We need to bring Christopher in on this. I haven't seen him this morning. Did he stay with his friends last night?"

Eben's eyes flicked to Erik and then back to Ashley. "Are you sure?"

"I'm sure. Can you go find him and bring him back here, please?"

Eben pushed his chair back. "I think I know where he is." Looking at Ashley, he said, "If you want to wait, I'll be back in twenty minutes."

She shook her head and smiled. "I'll be fine."

Eben hesitated, then stood and gave her shoulders a reassuring squeeze before turning and leaving the kitchen.

After he'd left, Erik asked, "What was that all about?"

"He just worries about me. He had a sister before the storm and I guess I'm her surrogate now."

"Christopher... Isn't that the kid from the bar last night?"

"The one you got into a fight with? Yes."

"Sorry about that. He and his friends looked like they were itching for a fight so I figured I'd oblige them, maybe teach them a lesson about messing with people they don't know."

"That you did," she said, smiling. "The way I heard it; they won't be harassing any more strangers anytime soon. At least, not anyone wearing a bearskin coat."

"He looked kind of young. Why do you think we need him in on this Mankato problem right now?"

"Yes, he's young. He just turned nineteen. But he's pretty sharp when it comes to strategy and planning. He's the reason you don't see any defenses around this place. We have them, you just don't see them."

"You're right about that," Erik said. "This place looks completely defenseless. I'm pretty sure Pierce thinks it is."

"That's Chris's strategy. We've had small raider groups come through every now and then over the years. They've always underestimated us and we've always either sent them packing or buried them."

"Unfortunately, Mankato isn't a small raiding party. I'd estimate twenty-five to thirty heavily armed men, probably more. From what I've seen, they're ruthless, determined, and experienced. I hope this Chris of yours doesn't underestimate *them*."

"I'm not expecting it to be easy but, between Chris and Eben, I'm sure they'll come up with something." She reached across the table and took his hands. "I don't know what your plans are, but if you could work with them and tell them everything you know about this Captain Pierce and his militia, it would help a lot. It would help all of us."

"Of course, I'll help. How can I say no to the belle of Belle Plaine? That would be like turning down a knighthood from the queen of England."

Ashley glanced down at the table and shook her head. "I don't think I'm royalty just yet." She took a breath, squeezing his hands, and then looked back up. "There's another reason I want Chris here." She paused, holding Erik's gaze with hers. "He's my son."

Erik's mind went blank for a minute. A son? He ran through what McClain had told him. He was sure he hadn't said anything about Ashley having a child. And Ashley had said that Eben was gay.

"You… and Ortiz?" he asked. "Not McClain. He never would have left."

Ashley smiled, looked down at the table again, and shook her head. When she looked back up at him, she was still smiling.

"There's that rusty intuition again." She gave his hands another firm squeeze. "Or should I say math skills. Think about it, Erik. He's nineteen years old." She paused, giving him time to do the calculation and then nodded when she saw the realization dawn on him.

"He's *our* son, Erik. Yours and mine. You're his father."

***

Pierce breathed a silent sigh of relief as the pickup truck rolled into the motor pool on time and intact. It steered around to the side of the field to avoid the duce-and-halves, Humvees, and other trucks parked near the entrance and then swung back around and crossed the center of the old football field, coming to a stop directly in front of him and Jules. It was drizzling rain but Pierce didn't give a crap and Jules wasn't complaining – he never complained. Pierce wanted a final report on Belle Plaine and he wanted it now.

Orlando and Vlad exited the truck.

"What's it look like?" Pierce asked before Orlando had even closed the driver's side door.

"Just like before," Orlando said, swinging the truck door shut. "Big farming community. Fields, livestock, three big greenhouses. A lot of people. They even have electricity and some kind of tavern or saloon."

"Defenses?"

"None that we could see. Road is rough but open all the way through to town. We didn't see a single lookout."

"Guns? Weapons?"

Orlando shook his head. "None that we could see, unless you want to count rakes and hoes as weapons." He pulled a pistol from his belt. "We did find this, though." He handed it to Pierce. "Found the previous truck about halfway up, wrecked in the ditch. Looked pretty bad. Front tire was shot out. The driver was killed in the wreck. The other was shot in the head."

Pierce took the gun and looked it over.

"Looks like Vern was telling the truth," Orlando said, "about the ambush."

"This doesn't prove anything," Pierce said, turning and handing the gun to Jules, who handed it to Vlad. "It wouldn't be hard to take out your own men and then concoct a story to fit the evidence. I don't suppose you saw that bastard up there, did you?"

"If he was there, he was laying low."

"Lying low or not, make sure everyone knows when we get to Belle Plaine, they have standing orders to shoot him on sight for desertion." He turned to Vlad. "Did you see any sign of this 'bear' character?"

Vlad shook his head. "No bear."

"We only watched the place for a few hours," Orlando said. "You didn't give us much time, but we didn't see anyone matching his description, and Vlad would have recognized him. If he was already there and warned them, it doesn't look like they took him seriously. Everyone was just going about their daily business from what we could see."

"Or he hasn't gotten there yet. The same standing order applies to the bear. He's to be shot on sight." Indicating the vehicles, he said, "I want these trucks refueled and ready to roll out again as soon as possible. If someone does get word to them, I don't want to give them any time to start thinking about blockading the road or putting up any kind of defense."

"How many trucks are we taking?" Orlando asked.

"All of them. I want every truck fueled, rearmed, and refit. Every man here is to be armed and ready to go the minute I give the word to roll out. I want to overwhelm that town with so much hardware and firepower they won't even think of resisting. We'll try to take it as intact as possible. But, if they resist, we're going to bring the hammer down and we're going to bring it down hard."

"Who's going to be on point?"

"I am. No offense to you or Vlad. I'm sure either of you could put this operation to bed without breaking a sweat, but I'm going to take the lead on this one. We've had too much shit in the wind lately and this is an important score. I'm not taking any chances. Once we take this town, I'm going to leave you and your pick of men in charge up there. You'll run it as both a supply center and our second base of operations."

Pierce raised his voice as though he was talking to a crowd now rather than just the three men standing with him.

"We're not raiders anymore, men. We're not cutting down cherry trees or killing the geese that lay the golden eggs. From now on we're conquerors. We're going to be rulers. Welcome to the new America, gentlemen. It starts right here, right now!"

***

Erik was sitting in a recliner in the living room while Ashley sat across from him on the couch when Eben returned with Chris. The seating arrangements were Ashley's idea. She didn't want to give Chris any impressions, right or wrong, before she had a chance to talk to him. She'd told Erik that she had, in fact, told the boy many years ago about his father. But Chris didn't know Erik's real name yet, or that Erik and the bear were one and the same.

He and Ashley had discussed how they would break the news to Chris that the man he'd picked a fight with last night was his father. Ashley felt it would be best if she did it alone and Erik agreed. He knew nothing about his son other than his name and that the kid could use some lessons in hand-to-hand combat and who not to pick fights with.

When Chris entered the room and saw Erik, his expression immediately turned surly. Erik didn't blame him. Chris had a black eye and his left cheek was red and swollen from where he had head-butted the kid last night.

"I believe you two have met," Eben said as a form of introduction.

Erik nodded, keeping his expression neutral. Chris gave him a scowl as he took a seat next to his mother.

"Does anyone want anything to drink?" Eben asked. "Water, tea, juice?" When no one answered, he added, "Double-shot of bourbon?"

Ashley shot him a warning look.

"I'm fine," Erik said.

"We should probably just get to it," Ashley said. She turned to Chris. "We just found out there's a group of raiders heading up our way from Mankato. There are a lot of them and they're heavily armed. They could be here anytime between now and next week."

"We've dealt with raiders before," Chris said, dismissively.

"Not any like these," Erik said. "These are more than just raiders. They're organized and experienced. They have working trucks as well as military weapons. They hit St. Peter south of here a few weeks ago. You took in some of their evacuees. I have it on good authority that they're

going to hit you even harder with a *blitzkrieg* type of attack, a lightning –
"

"– war," Chris interrupted. "Lightning war. I know what it means. It was a Nazi tactic in World War II. Hit the enemy fast and with overwhelming force."

Erik was impressed the kid would know about World War II. He let the interruption and snarky reply slide.

Eben took a seat on the adjacent couch. "You and your friends have been down to St. Peter, haven't you?" he asked Chris.

"We were down there last week. After that group came up here, we went down to have a look around. The place is completely burned out, empty."

"That was just a small attack," Erik said. "I doubt they used even half their forces there. Like I said, I have reason to believe he's going to hit you with a much larger force, maybe his entire militia."

"Who's 'he?'"

"He calls himself Captain Pierce. He's the head man down in Mankato. You mentioned World War II and the Nazis? Well, this guy is Hitler."

"You've met him?"

"I haven't met him personally," Erik said. "But I've been in Mankato. I've seen his men. I've seen his trucks and weapons. I was even in a small town west of Mankato when some of his men rolled in."

"How is it, then, that you're still alive?"

"I had the element of surprise. I killed three of them and the rest ran."

"Well shit," Chris said, grinning and looking back and forth between Eben and Ashley. "Maybe we don't need to do anything. Hell, we've got *the bear* on our side. He can just…"

"Shut up, Chris," Ashley said.

"How do you know he's heading this way?" Eben asked for Chris's benefit. Erik had already explained it to both him and Ashley.

"An old friend of mine told me. He's kind of a reluctant member of that group. He's the one who sent me up here to warn you."

"But how do you *know* they're coming?" Chris asked.

"Chris…," Ashley said, sounding exasperated.

"I'm serious," Chris said. "I mean, who is this guy?" He indicated Erik. "What do we know about him, other than people call him the bear and he wears a smelly old coat. For all we know, he's just fucking with us, or he's trying to work some angle of his own."

"I think we can trust what he says," Eben said. "That 'old friend' he referred to is Corporal McClain. I'm sure your mother has mentioned him before."

"They've already sent one scouting party," Erik said. "I stopped them on the road before they got here. But I'm sure by now Pierce has sent another. McClain seemed to think he is pretty serious about taking this place. He said they'll be heading this way within a week or two, maybe sooner."

"So, what we need now is some kind of plan," Ashley said. "You and your friends are in charge of security and defense. What can you come up with and how quickly can you do it?"

Chris was silent for a moment, thinking. Erik could understand the kid was probably a bit overwhelmed. Here he was, used to providing defense against small groups of clumsy raiders and the occasional scavenger. Now he was being asked to come up with a plan to repel a small army equipped with vehicles and heavy weapons. And he had just a matter of days to do it.

Chris's gaze flicked to Erik a couple of times while he was pondering and then back to Ashley.

"Why does he keep staring at me?"

Ashley suppressed a grin. "He just spends most of his time in the woods." She gave Erik a look. "I guess he's not used to being around people."

Chris thought a moment and then glanced back to Erik.

"Will they be coming from the south? Straight up the highway?"

"Most likely. He doesn't think you have anything in the way of defenses. And if he did send another scouting party, they saw the same things I did. This place looks wide open, easy pickings. He'll probably do like he always does and roll his trucks right up the highway and straight into town. He calls himself a captain but McClain said he doesn't have any real military experience."

Chris looked down at the floor, nodding his head. Finally, he said, "Okay. I've got a couple of ideas, but I want to think on them a bit, do a little research."

They waited but he didn't say anything more.

"Care to enlighten us?" Eben prompted.

"I'd rather not say any more with him here." Chris nodded to Erik. "You say we can trust him but I don't know him. For all I know he's working with this Pierce character, trying to find out how we'll defend ourselves. If I were going to attack another town, that's what I'd do –

send a spy in to 'warn' them and then learn all about their defensive plans."

"Chris...," Ashley started in another exasperated tone.

"No, he's right," Erik said. "McClain told me that Pierce has spies everywhere. Hell, McClain himself is sort of a spy, a saboteur working against Pierce. For all anyone knows, I could be a spy for Mankato. And there's no reason for me to know your plans. I just came here to warn you and I've done that. The rest is up to you." He stood up. "You guys discuss it. Have a town meeting or whatever. Decide what you're going to do. I'll hang around awhile just to let you know I'm not running back to report to Pierce."

"Where are you going?" Ashley asked.

"I haven't really seen much of your town yet. Figured I'd just wander around, see the sights." He turned to leave.

"I'll go with you," Eben said, also standing. "Give you the guided tour. Make sure you don't have a radio hidden somewhere." He looked at Ashley. "You and Chris have a lot to discuss. If you need us, come out and give a holler. Otherwise, we'll be back later."

"Is that okay?" Erik asked, getting the gist of what Eben was telling her. "Or do you want me to stay?"

"You go on," she said. "Eben, show him what we've accomplished here. Chris and I will be fine." She patted Chris's hand.

Chris frowned, glancing back and forth between them, as though he had a feeling he was missing something.

***

"We've got over a hundred and eighty people here now," Eben said as he and Erik walked between the small farming plots and livestock pens. "We're pretty self-sufficient. I don't think anyone here has opened a tin can or box of stale pasta in years."

"What about stuff you can't grow?" Erik asked. "Salt, sugar, soap, fuel... stuff like that?"

"We're not one hundred percent self-sufficient yet but we're getting there. We grow beets and corn and process them for sugar. Soap, we make ourselves the old-fashioned way, with lye from wood ashes and rendered animal fat. Salt is pretty plentiful. We are in Minnesota, after all. We found a warehouse where they stored several hundred tons of it for the roads. As for fuel, there's plenty in underground tanks and we use a stabilizer to get it to burn decently. As you probably noticed in the tavern, we have a still for making alcohol. We're working on a larger version for when we get some of our generators converted over from gasoline."

They came to a hog pen and stood at the fence, watching about twenty hogs root in the soil for edible treats. A few chickens darted in between them, pecking at the dirt the hogs turned over.

"So, everyone just pitches in and works for the benefit of all?"

Eben laughed. "Yes, it's socialism at its finest. You work, you eat. If you can't work, we'll find something else you can do."

"So, why did Chris ask me at the bar how I intended to pay for my beer?"

"He was just messing with you. The beer is like everything else here. As long as you're working, feel free to have a pint or a couple of shots."

"Doesn't anyone ever overdo it? Take more than what they put in?"

"Newcomers sometimes. There's no punishment for it. But peer pressure and guilt can be powerful motivators to get with the program."

"And if they don't?"

Eben grinned. "You're really trying to find the cracks in the system, aren't you? Yes, there are cracks here and there. No system is perfect but we learn as we go. As far as someone who refuses to play by the rules, there's really nothing we can do but escort them out of town and tell them good luck. But we haven't had a problem with that yet."

Erik stood watching the hogs and chickens, thinking about it.

"Do you think it can last? I mean as you grow?"

"No, probably not. Eventually, we'll have to make changes. We'll need laws, rules, some form of real government someday if we keep growing. Maybe even – God forbid – some sort of currency. And then it's right back to the old civilization, which, as I remember, wasn't all that civil in the first place."

He looked up at the sky and Erik followed his gaze. It was dark to the south, probably raining. Here, there were just a few wispy, high-altitude clouds and plenty of sunshine.

"But I don't think we'll get that far," Eben continued. "This is like the calm before the storm. We're doing fine now, but winter is coming, one final great winter that will last for centuries. In another ten, twenty years, everything we've built here may be buried under a hundred feet of snow and ice."

"But you've got plans to move south."

"We do. Ashley, God bless her, has a lot of faith in me and that I'll be able to pull it off." He shook his head. "I'll do my best, but it's not going to be easy. With this many people now, it's not going to be easy at all."

"You two are really close, aren't you?"

"We are. I love her and would do anything for her. But I'm sure she's told you there's nothing physical between us."

Erik nodded.

"I think Corporal McClain was in love with her too," Eben said. "But I don't think she was interested in any sort of relationship at the time. That's probably why she got close to me. I was safe." He looked at Erik. "You know she hasn't been involved – physically, I mean – with any man since you left, don't you?"

"No, she didn't really say and I didn't ask."

"She's a tough one to get close to, Erik. A lot of men have tried. But you... I don't know how you did it, but she saw something in you and she let you inside. And she's never let you go –" He tapped his chest. "– in here. That's got to count for something."

He didn't say anything. Since this morning, he'd finally come to the realization that he was in love with her, probably always had been. But it had never occurred to him that she might also be in love with him.

"Do you think you're going to stay with us?" Eben asked. "However this all plays out, do you think you'd be able to finally settle down and start a new life here with us? With her?"

He thought about it. He'd been thinking about it all day.

"Honestly, I can't tell you. I didn't even know she was here. My plan was to warn you about Mankato and then just fade back into the woods. I've spent more than half my life there, alone and away from people. That's really my home now. But now I've found her again. And this morning I found out I'm a father." He shook his head. "It's like that morning after the storm all over again. My whole world has been changed in a single night and I don't know what to do, which way to go."

"What did you do after the storm?"

"I just made up my mind to keep moving forward. I'd made a promise to my sister that I would come back to her. I guess I latched onto that promise, used it as my compass. It was my motivation to keep moving forward despite all obstacles."

"You followed your heart. It wasn't the promise that kept you moving forward. It's too easy to make a promise. People do it all the time. It was your love for your sister. She was your compass."

"I've loved other people too," Erik said. "But they're gone now."

Eben put his hand on his shoulder.

"I know of one that isn't. She's back there in that house right now. She's warm and alive and she has both of our hearts."

***

Ashley stood in the kitchen, holding her cup of tea and looking out the window, watching Chris as he walked across the yard and the road, heading toward the horse pen where Erik was leaning forward on the fence, staring out across the pasture.

"How did it go?" Eben asked, coming into the kitchen behind her.

"Surprisingly well," she said, not turning from the window. "He was a little shocked at first. That's understandable. But he seemed to recover quickly. He said he needs to think about it, let it sink in."

"It is a lot to take in all at once, to suddenly find out you're the son of a legend, a rumor... a cave man."

She laughed. "Believe it or not, I really think he kind of suspected what I had to tell him. Maybe he has some of his father's old intuition." She turned and sat with Eben at the table. "He wants to talk to him. After all, all he knows about his father is what I've told him, and those stories are twenty years old. Just those and anecdotes about the bear he's heard in the tavern. He wants to know *who* his father really is, not what people say he is or what they say he's done."

"Sounds like he got not only his father's intuition but also his mother's good sense."

She took a sip of her tea and asked, "Do you think he'll stay?"

"Do you want him to stay?"

She looked down at her tea and sighed. "I want him to be happy, to be at peace. He's been through a lot. I can see it in his eyes every time I look at him. Even when he's smiling, there's sadness there. I think he's lost a lot more people in his life than we know, done things he's not proud of and will never tell anyone."

"I see it too," Eben said. "The sadness and the secrets. He's conflicted now. He didn't know you were here in Belle Plaine. He came here to warn us about Mankato and then fade back into his forest. But now he's found you again and he just found out he has a son." He shook his head. "That's a lot to absorb, maybe even more than Chris finding out he has a bear for a father."

"I know he's afraid he'll lose me, lose us," Ashley said, "just like he lost his sister and so many others along the way. He thinks death and misery follow him."

"Can you blame him?"

She stood and went back to the window. Chris had joined Erik at the fence. They were both looking out at the horses, talking.

Eben came up behind her and wrapped his arms around her.

"He loves you, you know. He asked me what he should do. I told him to follow his heart, just like he's always done. I guess we'll have to wait and see where it leads him." He squeezed her tighter and kissed the top of her head.

"I hope he chooses you over those smelly old coyotes."

"Me too."

***

Erik had always wondered what it would be like to ride a horse. He thought it would be a little scary, to have such a powerful animal under his control. What if it decided it didn't want him on its back anymore? He'd heard of people getting their necks broken by being bucked off or getting their skulls cracked open by one of those hooves. What would it be like sitting atop such a large and powerful animal that could kill you on a whim?

As he watched the horses mill about the pasture, his thoughts stole back to the one that had killed Seth. Well, the horse really hadn't killed him. It had been the fence wire. They were just trying to release the horse from its pen. It had been nothing more than a freak accident, not the horse's fault.

No good deed goes unpunished, he thought. It was an unwritten rule he had lived by since losing April. It was one of the reasons he had avoided people for so long.

He wondered if that damn horse finally found water and if it was still alive somewhere. How long did horses live, anyway?

He heard someone coming up behind him. He assumed it was Eben returning but then Chris joined him at the fence.

Chris leaned on the fence next to him and looked out over the horses. After a while he said, "We've got three new foals this year. They're in a pen down on the south side."

"I saw that. Before I came in last night, I kind of spied on this place through binoculars for a while. Figure it's always good to know what you're walking into."

Chris grinned. "You certainly walked into it alright. Sorry about that thing at the bar by the way. We were just being stupid."

"Sorry about the eye. I didn't know you were Ashley's son. I guess I'm lucky she didn't kick my ass for that. She once threatened to throw me off a balcony for a lot less."

Chris laughed. "She told me about that. Back at the mansion, right? Just before you were attacked by that religious cult."

Erik nodded and then realized he'd just admitted to being the young man Ashley knew at the mansion, the man whom she'd told Chris was his father. And he hadn't questioned it.

"So, she told you? Who I am?"

"That she knew you back in Elk River?" Chris nodded. "She told me a long time ago that you were my father but I only knew your name. And the stories, of course. She said she only knew you for a few days but you must have made quite an impression. She said you left to keep a promise to your sister. She never knew what happened to you or if you would return someday." He looked at Erik. "And now here you are, twenty years later. It's kind of a lot, you know, finding out your father is this larger-than-life figure, this legend you've heard people tell stories about all your life."

"I should have come back earlier," Erik said. "If I had known…"

"It's just the way it was. I don't blame you. Hell, you were what, fifteen years old? She was nineteen? And you were five hundred miles from home. Jesus, the world had just ended. Billions of people were dead in a single night. Nothing worked anymore. Cities were burning. There were corpses everywhere, crazy people running around shooting each other…" He shook his head. "Mom told me about how they spent months going from house to house removing all the corpses and burning them."

He looked back up and gazed out at the horses.

"I've seen the ruins of some of the big cities like Minneapolis. I can only imagine what it was like, before and after. You go to bed one night surrounded by millions of people, bright lights, cell phones, televisions, refrigerators, cars… and the next morning you wake up to nothing, just a dead, silent world. Mom said some people killed themselves. I don't know what I would have done."

"I think you would have survived. Like I did. Like your mother."

"So, what do I call you? Dad? Erik? Bear?"

"I wasn't there to be a father to you. Hell, I was a kid myself. You're probably lucky I wasn't around. I imagine Eben has been more of a father to you than I ever could have been. Between him and Ashley, I think they did alright with you."

"You're right," Chris said. "It would feel a little weird calling you Dad. I don't even call Eben that. So, I guess Erik it is. Unless you prefer Bear."

He chuckled, shaking his head. "That damn old man. He hung that name around my neck back when I was about seventeen. Now I guess I'm stuck with it."

"It suits you. It really does."

They both went back to watching the horses.

"So," Chris said after a while, "have you decided whether or not you're going to hang around? "

"Eben asked me that too. Let's just take it one day at a time for now. We've still got the problem with Mankato to deal with. If you've come up with something that'll get everyone here safely through that, then ask me again when it's all over."

"Fair enough." Chris pushed back from the fence. "Let's go to the storage shed. I think we have some stuff there that might bring back some old memories."

Your mother has already brought back plenty of those, Erik thought as he turned and followed Chris.

They walked down the road past several farming plots and some more livestock pens to the grounds of an old high school. Chris explained the grounds around the school were now being used to grow hay and oats for the livestock. They crossed through the field and went around to the gymnasium behind the school building.

"Not exactly what I'd call a shed," Erik commented as he followed Chris to the front doors.

"We did use a shed at first," Chris said, holding one of the doors open for him. "But as Belle Plaine grew, we had to find a bigger building. I guess the name just stuck."

Inside, the gymnasium had been converted into a series of large rooms running down both sides of the floor. Chris gave him a tour, showing him storage rooms for hay, oats, corn, beets, potatoes, carrots, onions, and even a couple of refrigerated rooms storing a large variety of cheeses and smoked meats.

"We've been working on a second storage building," Chris said as they walked down the center aisle. "Come fall, this place fills up pretty quick and we don't want to run the risk of losing everything we've worked for in a fire or other mishap."

Erik was impressed, but he was still wondering how any of this could help them defend this place against Pierce and his men.

Chris finally rounded a corner and bent down to pull open a panel in the floor.

"Here's what we came to see. Down here."

Erik followed him down the narrow flight of steps to a short hallway leading to a large utility room. When Chris opened the door and flipped on the lights, Erik found himself instantly transported back to the rec room of the mansion in Elk River.

"Holy shit," he exclaimed. "You brought everything from the mansion. And then some!"

The room was filled wall to wall with racks of rifles, shotguns, and pistols, many of them military issue. Rows of steel shelves down the center held cases of ammunition and cans of gunpowder and fuel. There were several cases of dynamite and C-4, blasting caps, det-cord, and other explosives. With these were spools of wire, plunger-type detonators, Kevlar helmets, body armor, binoculars, canteens… the works.

"We may be a bunch of farmers," Chris said, grinning, "but that doesn't mean we're defenseless. Believe it or not, this is just one of two armories we have."

"Jesus Christ," Erik said, walking down one side of the room, looking everything over. "This is more than we had at the mansion, way more. Where'd you get all this stuff?"

"We've been adding to it little by little over time. A lot of it came from one of those armories Eben mentioned. And whenever we go out to one of the surrounding towns, we keep our eyes open. Best we grab it before scavengers or raiders do. Seems you lived in a pretty heavily armed society before the storm."

"Yeah, we did. But damn! To see it all together in one place…"

"Now you know why I was a little hesitant to tell you our plans. You said this Pierce character thinks we're defenseless. Best to let him think we'll be defending ourselves with rakes and pitchforks."

Erik turned to Chris. "Don't tell me you're thinking of going against him head-to-head. They're ruthless and have a lot of experience in crushing resistance."

"Not a chance," Chris said. "That's medieval and stupid." He took a hand grenade off a shelf and looked at it thoughtfully. "Winters around here can be pretty long and awful damn boring. I also collect books. I've spent a lot of long winters reading about the history of the old world, especially about your wars and military battles, about the tactics and strategies different armies have used over the centuries."

"Your mom said you were good at strategy and defense. What have you got in mind?"

Chris tossed the grenade to him.

"Have you ever heard of the Battle of Agincourt? Or maybe a little place called Thermopylae and the battle of the three hundred?"

MAY 24

Erik was leaning back against the fence, looking up at the stars in the clear, night sky when Ashley came up beside him and took his arm in hers. She snuggled up close to him.

"Hey, stranger. What are you doing out here all by yourself?"

"Just looking at the stars."

"I'd think you see them every night, sleeping out in the woods."

"I do, but that doesn't mean I ever get tired of looking at them." He leaned over and gave her a quick peck on the top of the head. "So, how did the meeting go?"

"You could have been there, you know. They wouldn't have chased you away with pitchforks and burning torches."

"Now you tell me."

"It went well. Eben and Chris did a good job of explaining the situation and getting everyone on board."

"I just thought my presence there might have been a little distracting."

"You're probably right. If you were there, everyone would have been looking at you instead of being focused on what Chris and Eben had to say. I think they did a good job of emphasizing the danger without panicking anyone. We've had to deal with small raiding parties before so that helped."

"Pierce and his men won't be a small raiding party."

"They know that. Trust me. Christopher will not underestimate them. And those people we took in from St. Peter, they helped underscore how serious this threat is."

Across the field in the direction of town, an enormous, bright yellow-orange ball of fire suddenly lit up the night sky and rose high into the air. It was followed by the *whoomph* of an explosion and the sounds of maybe forty or fifty people cheering and hollering.

"What in the hell was that?" Erik asked, remembering the last time he'd seen such a fireball. It had been twenty years ago, back in Aitkin, when Crazy Bob destroyed a truck stop and himself.

Ashley laughed. "That's just Chris and his friends. They do that every now and then after they've collected enough old cell phones and computers. The batteries in them are highly volatile and it doesn't take much to set them off."

"I was wondering about that," Erik said, remembering Chris and his friends with their bag of cell phones.

"Such is our entertainment now," Ashley sighed. "Remember when we used to veg out on television, play video games, or surf the web for hours at a time? I remember my sister couldn't stray more than two feet from her cell phone. Now we ignite piles of batteries from all that old technology and think it's pretty cool."

They watched the brilliant, distant glow and listened to the people cheering and laughing for a while. Erik had to admit, in the absence of anything else, it was probably pretty entertaining, especially if there was a lot of alcohol involved, which he was sure there was.

"So why did you name him Christopher?" he asked.

"A little late to be debating baby names, don't you think?"

"I was just curious."

"It was actually Saundra who suggested it. Her and Sergeant Ortiz. They were both Catholic, you know."

"No, actually I never really thought about it. I figured they were both religious but I didn't ask any questions."

"Saint Christopher is the patron saint of travelers."

"Hmmm..." He didn't get it.

Ashley punched him lightly on the arm. "We chose that name because of you, you big, furry galoot. You were the traveler."

"Ahhhhh...!" He said, a little more enthusiastically to indicate he really did get it this time.

"We kind of figured you could use all the help you could get."

He put his arm around her shoulders. "Must have worked. I'm still here."

"What's that?" she asked, seeing the silver chain in his other hand.

He let the blue amethyst rabbit drop and dangle by its chain. It sparkled by the light of the distant fire.

"Magic bunny. That's what Sam called it. It was her favorite piece of jewelry."

He put the necklace and pendent in her hand.

She turned it over in her fingers. "It's pretty." Looking at the chain, she saw it was broken. "You know, we have a guy here in town who works with metal. I'm sure he could fix this for you."

"Can he make it bear-proof? That's how it got broken."

"I don't know about bear-proof but he's pretty good." She slipped the rabbit off the chain and went to hand it back to Erik.

"Keep it with the chain," he said. "I trust you."

Ashley put the rabbit and chain in her pocket.

She moved to stand in front of him and then leaned back against his chest. He wrapped his arms around her and they watched the glow from across the field for several minutes. The battery bonfire was slowly dying down, as was the noise from the crowd gathered to watch it.

"About six years ago," Erik said, "I was up north of here. It was late spring. The leaves were out and there were blossoms on the trees. I was tracking a heard of deer I'd seen earlier when I found myself on the side of this hill overlooking a small, incredibly clear lake. It was surrounded by hills on all sides, hidden in the forest. There were no dead trees leftover from the storm. It was like the whole area had been missed. There was a stream on one end that came out of the hills and made a small waterfall in this little cove. All around it were cottonwood trees and the air was filled with their seeds. You know, those white, cottony ones that float on the air and look like snow. It was just so incredible to come out of the woods and suddenly find myself looking out on something like that. It took my breath away. I sat down on that hillside and stayed there all day, clear to sunset. I didn't want to miss a minute of it."

"It sounds beautiful."

"It was. I remember thinking it looked like the one spot on Earth never touched by man. But the thing I remember most while I was sitting there... I remember wishing I had someone to share it with."

Ashley turned and looked up at him, meeting his eyes.

"I remember wishing you were there with me," he said.

She took his head in her hands and gently pulled his face to hers and kissed him.

"You don't have to say anything, but I want you to know in case I never get another chance. I love you, Erik."

He wrapped his arms around her and pulled her closer.

"I do have to say it, because I may never get another chance either. I love you too. I always have."

MAY 28

Damn, he looked sharp.

Pierce turned to one side and then the other, checking his uniform in the full-length mirror. He was wearing a military dress uniform, complete with colonel's insignia, newly polished boots, black leather belt, service pistol, and a chest-full of ribbons and medals. It made him think he should have joined the military when he was younger instead of becoming a postal worker. The wonders he might have accomplished.

He had finally decided to promote himself to full colonel. He held off doing it earlier in deference to the civilians of Mankato. God knew why, but they had loved Colonel Bates. But that was over and he was fully in charge now, with McClain having been exposed as the traitor he was. He'd thought about promoting himself to general but colonel sounded better.

In the mirror, he could see Jules, Orlando, and Vlad waiting on him. In the street outside were two deuce-and-halves, men, munitions, and five pickup trucks. Each pickup had a fifty-caliber machine gun mounted in the bed. Besides the men in this room, there were twenty-three more waiting on the street outside, all fully armed and ready to follow him to victory.

Going up against a bunch of farmers – this was going to be a cakewalk. He almost wished the dirt-grubbers had some weapons to put up a fight with. It would make his coming victory that much more heroic and worthy of future history.

He took his glass of whiskey from the table and downed what was left in one gulp. Sure, it was nine or ten in the morning, but fuck it. He made the rules now. He set the glass down and turned to the men in the room.

"Okay, how are we looking? Is everything ready to roll?"

Orlando nodded. "Ready, sir. All men are present and accounted for except Vern. Still no sign of him."

Pierce liked that "sir" Orlando had thrown in. He was going to have to make that mandatory for the rest of his men. But he was still pissed about Vern's middle-of-the-night escape.

"Like I told you earlier," Pierce said, "if anyone sees him along the way, he's to be shot on sight. That order still stands. But if he's in Belle

Plaine, we'll arrest him and bring him back here for execution. I don't want someone thinking they see him in a crowd and opening fire. I don't want a firefight if we can avoid it. Is that understood?"

All three men nodded. Orlando was the only one to say, "Yes, sir."

"We're going into a farming community with few if any weapons. They may have been warned that we're coming and they may try to put up some kind of resistance, but I want as little shooting as possible. Yes, we're going in heavy, but that's mostly for intimidation. I want to take this place as intact as possible. It will be a vital resource and second center of operations. No one, and I mean no one, fires unless fired upon or unless I order it. And even then, you target the people, not the buildings or the livestock. Is that *clearly* understood?"

More nods. One "Yes, sir."

"Good. We do this right, men, and we're well on our way to rebuilding America. These towns and villages out there, they're all struggling to survive without any real leadership or any form of government. We're going to provide both for them. They may resist at first, but they will come to see the wisdom in what we do. We will unite them under one banner and we will lead them into a new age."

His gaze moved from one man to the other. They were his lieutenants. They would enforce his rule.

"Are there any questions?"

Orlando stepped forward. "Sir. Just to be clear, what do we do if we come across the bear? Arrest and execution like Vern or shoot on sight?"

He felt a sudden surge of anger. God, he was getting sick of hearing that son of a bitch's name. He turned to Vlad.

"If the bear is still in town and shows his face, I want you, personally, to take him out. Challenge him to a fight and then cut his head off. I want it to be a goddamn spectacle. Use his skull as a soup bowl, a candy dish, a toilet... I don't care."

Vlad gripped the handle of the battle ax in his belt and nodded, grinning broadly and showing a mouthful of stained, oversized teeth.

Pierce adjusted his uniform and belt, feeling sharp and in charge.

"Let's roll!"

***

Peering through the spotting scope from atop one of the old grain silos, Erik guessed he could see at least twenty miles down the highway, maybe thirty. It was a perfect vantage point to watch for anyone approaching from the south. The highway was already broken up and overgrown, but Eben and half a dozen men from town had been out the past couple of days breaking it up even more. Not enough to be suspicious, but enough to slow a convoy of trucks down to little more than a crawl. Erik estimated from the time they first caught sight of Pierce's approaching army, they would have around twenty to thirty minutes to alert the town and get ready.

There were other vantage points set up to the north and east, anywhere Pierce's militia might be able to enter town if he decided to split his forces or approach from a different direction. Erik didn't think that was likely though, given what he'd heard about Pierce. Chris and Eben agreed. The man was arrogant, over-confident, and lacking any actual military training or experience. Chances were good he was going to roll straight into town from the south.

Erik had never heard of Agincourt or Thermopylae. Chris explained they were examples of how a smaller, weaker force could defeat a much larger, stronger army simply by choosing *where* to fight. After Chris laid out his plan, Erik had to agree with Ashley. His son had a definite knack for strategy. His plan was risky. A dozen different things could go wrong and a lot of people could get killed, especially if Pierce split his forces or came in from the wrong direction. But if it worked, there was a very good chance they would never have to worry about Pierce or Mankato ever again.

He turned from the spotting scope and looked back out over the fields and town they were preparing to defend. The threat of frost was past and there was a dozen or more people in the fields today, turning the soil with shovels, hoes, and rakes, readying the ground for planting. He had pitched in yesterday after his watch, grabbing a spade and working until evening. He thought he was in pretty good shape, but the hard farm labor proved him wrong. This morning, he was aching in muscles and joints he never knew he had.

A little to the east, three people on horses were herding about twenty cattle from one pasture to another. Four men were repairing a fence out by the road, and the sound of hammering was coming from somewhere in town as repairs were made to winter-damaged homes. To an outside observer, there was nothing indicating the town was either aware of or preparing for an armed invasion. The deception was deliberate. Erik hoped it would work.

He turned at the sound of shoes on the metal ladder leading up the outside of the grain silo. Chris appeared and joined him atop the observation post.

"Mom's got lunch ready any time you want to take a break," he said, sitting beside Erik. "I'll take over for a while." He looked at Erik's much shorter hair and neatly trimmed beard. "Whoa! I see Mom finally chased you down with the scissors."

"Needed it anyway," Erik said, running his hand over his beard. "All I've ever had to trim it with is my knife. Guess I'm lucky she didn't shave it all off."

"Makes you look more civilized. Not much but a little."

Erik glanced back across the fields and to the town again, remembering something he'd been wanting to ask about.

"Why are there no children around here?"

Chris shrugged. "I don't know. There just aren't. As far as I know, I'm the youngest person in town."

Erik considered it. He hadn't seen children in any village or town for a long time.

"From what I've seen," Chris added, seeming to anticipate his thoughts, "there aren't any children in any of the surrounding towns, either. People talk about it sometimes, mostly among themselves. Most people think it has something to do with that storm. Mom told me about it. Maybe it not only killed off ninety percent of the people, but it also might have made it so the survivors can't have children anymore."

"Not all of the survivors," Erik said. "You're here."

"Eben has a theory about that. He figures maybe since ninety percent of the people were killed by the storm, maybe about ninety percent of the survivors are sterile. He thinks you and Mom fall into the small percentage of people who can still have kids. And either by fate or some blind stroke of luck, you two found each other."

"Sounds reasonable. I don't know about this whole 'fate' thing but I remember there were some people who were affected to a greater or lesser degree. Some people took a long time to die. I guess most of those who survived still got a small dose of the radiation or whatever it was, not enough to make them sick but just enough to make them sterile."

"That's his theory," Chris said. "He admits he's no biologist or anything, but it seems to be the only reasonable theory in town. I've heard others say they think it's divine judgment or whatever, but that doesn't make much sense. If that were true, wouldn't all of the religious people who survived be able to have kids?"

"I've given up trying to figure out what happened and what's going to happen.   But if people aren't able to have kids anymore, this civilization you're trying to rebuild isn't going to last very long."

"Maybe not, but that doesn't mean we're going to sit back and accept it."

His defiance of fate reminded Erik of something Ashley once said.

"Do not go gentle into that good night. Rage, rage against the dying of the light."

"That sounds like something Mom would say."

"She did. I think it's from one of those old books she likes to quote. There's more but I can't remember it all."

Chris peered through the spotting scope. A moment later he looked back up and out into the distance.

"Maybe you scared them off." He glanced back to Erik. "You don't fuck with the bear. That's what they say."

"I really doubt I scared them off. *Pissed* them off, maybe. Now, you have Eben grow his hair longer, dress him in leather, and give him a sword and shield… That would put the fear of God into anybody."

Chris laughed. "Yeah, I can definitely see Eben as some ancient warrior wading into battle and hacking off heads. He'd certainly scare the hell out of me."

Erik laughed with him and then stood up, feeling his knees pop from having sat for so long.

"Okay. I'm going to go see what your mom has for lunch. I'm thinking it may be another day or two before they show up, maybe even a week, but keep watching anyway."

He was swinging his foot over the edge of the silo to step onto the ladder when Chris peered through the scope again.

"Hold on," Chris said, suddenly serious. "Looks like you didn't scare them off after all."

***

Ashley was shaving slices of roast beef onto a plate when Eben came into the kitchen and crossed to the sink to wash his hands.

"Are we having a party?" he asked, glancing at the towering pile of beef on the plate, the large block of cheese, and the stack of bread slices.

"I've discovered Erik is a man of very large appetite. He puts even you to shame."

Eben shook the water off his hands and picked up a towel.

"He can drink me under the table too. I swear that man can put away a gallon of beer as easily as a glass of water."

"And just when were you two out drinking? Was Christopher with you?"

He came up behind her and wrapped his arms around her waist, hugging her lightly.

"What's this for?" she asked, setting her knife down and rubbing his arms.

"You. Right then you sounded so... I don't know. Domestic. So motherly. I don't think I've ever seen you this contented."

She closed her eyes and leaned her head back against his broad chest.

"I am. I've got three wonderful men under my roof now, all brave, strong, and handsome. I wish it could always be like this."

The sound of three distant, sharp whistles came through the open kitchen window. The prearranged warning was repeated and quickly picked up by others in town. Soon, the air was filled with whistles, shouts, and the sounds of people running.

Ashley felt her heart drop.

***

The broken, overgrown pavement forced the convoy to move at an agonizingly slow pace. Pierce considered ordering Orlando to drive faster. These slow, heavy bumps and thuds as the truck crawled over broken slabs of concrete were like a kind of water torture. The anticipation of the next bump was worse than the bump itself.

"This is different," Orlando said warily. "I don't remember the road being this bad."

"We're in a heavier truck," Pierce said. "Probably makes the bumps feel worse."

Pierce and Orlando were in one of the two deuce-and-halves. Burrows and Furman were leading the way ahead of them in one of the pickup trucks. Behind them were most of the other working vehicles in Mankato's fleet. Pierce had wanted to throw his entire fleet and all of his men at Belle Plaine but Orlando talked him into holding some back at the last moment. While he rarely tolerated dissenting opinions, he had to admit sometimes Orlando's suggestions were at least worth considering.

After another series of bone-jarring thuds, Orlando suddenly braked and brought the truck to a halt, almost rear-ending the truck ahead of them.

"What the hell's going on?" Pierce demanded. He could see some brush blocking the road ahead but nothing the trucks couldn't drive through. "Why are we stopping?"

"I don't know," Orlando said. "I'll find out." He opened his door and got out.

"God damn it," Pierce growled. He flung his door open and followed Orlando around to the driver's side door of the lead truck.

Furman, driver of the lead truck, said nothing. He simply pointed down the road ahead of him.

A large piece of plywood was propped up against a pile of brush and tree limbs in the center of the road. Painted on the plywood in large, block letters was a simple message.

MANKATO
NO QUARTER GIVEN BEYOND THIS POINT
TURN BACK NOW

"Looks like they've been warned," Orlando said, gazing past the sign and farther down the road. "Probably the bear."

"It's bullshit," Pierce scoffed, "a pathetic plea for mercy is all. What the hell does that mean anyway? No quarter."

"It means they'll shoot first if we get close enough, and it won't be a warning shot."

Pierce laughed. "Seriously? Do they even *know* what we're bringing down on them? Jesus, they've just told us what they're going to do. Tell everyone to get ready. If these assholes want to dance, let's oblige them."

"Maybe we should split up," Orlando suggested. "Come at them from different directions." He glanced to the west. "We could take three trucks…"

"Screw that. We're not splitting up to give them smaller targets to pick off. We're going in full force." Pierce turned to the men who'd gotten out of the trucks behind them and were standing on the road.

"Everyone back in your trucks now," he shouted. "Machine gunners get ready. Lock and load. Move it!"

As the convoy started forward again, rolling over the brush pile and splintering the plywood sign beneath its wheels, Pierce used his binoculars to scan the road ahead of them. The lead truck was causing problems with his field of view, but either Burrows or Furman would also be watching for trouble.

They were coming to a narrow gap where the road cut through a thick growth of trees. Beyond that, Pierce finally got his first glimpse of Belle Plaine.

"Are you kidding me?" Pierce exclaimed as he stared through the binoculars.

"What?"

"They're out working in the fields! They're out there just hoeing and raking and shit." He brought his binoculars down and turned to Orlando, grinning with disbelief. "It's just another day on the farm for them. They've got no idea we're coming. These morons must have thought their pathetic warning sign would work." He raised his binoculars and peered ahead again, chuckling to himself. "Jesus, we might not even have to waste a single bullet."

As the trucks rolled into the gap, the heavy woods closed in on either side of the road. Pierce lost sight of the town and lowered his binoculars again. He turned back to Orlando.

"First thing we do is get everyone rounded up, find their leader. I'm sure they have one. We let them know –"

The air was suddenly filled with deafening, thunderous detonations from all around. Great clouds of dirt and large chunks of pavement were flying up from both sides of the road. Every windshield in the truck exploded and Pierce felt the sharp cubes of safety glass slicing into his head, face, and neck.

The lead truck with Burrows and Furman was lifted into the air by one of the explosions and was flipping backwards toward them. Orlando cranked the steering wheel hard to the left. The duce-and-half skidded sideways and began to tip over. Burrow's truck cartwheeled over where they had been and crashed down onto the truck behind them. Orlando fought the wheel, now cranking it to the right, trying to keep the big truck from rolling, but another blast almost directly beneath them lifted it and pitched it over.

Pierce squeezed his eyes shut and gritted his teeth, trying to find anything to hold onto as they rolled over and over before coming to a jarring stop against a tree.

Broken glass, dirt, and debris were raining down on him while the thunderous roar of more explosions and the screeching of tires and metal filled the air outside. Fighting the blackness that was closing in on him, a single thought kept repeating itself over and over in Pierce's head like a broken record.

No quarter given…

***

"Holy shit!" Erik exclaimed, raising his head as the carnage finally began to subside. Dirt, rocks, and splinters of wood were raining down on them. He glanced to Eben. "Think you used enough explosives there, hoss?"

They were lying flat on the ground about twenty yards inside the tree line along the southeast side of the road. Spread out to their left and right were thirty-odd men and women, all armed with rifles and shotguns. Chris, Ashley, and another thirty armed men and women were in the trees on the other side of the road. They had left about twenty villagers working in and around the fields to give the impression of a wholly unprepared farming community. The deception seemed to have worked.

"Blame your son," Eben said. "He's the one with the go-big-or-go-home philosophy."

A one-hundred-yard stretch of highway had been mined along both sides of the road where the trees closed in and allowed no escape. Sticks of dynamite and bricks of plastic explosive were all wired together and set to go off in two series of cascading blasts from front to back, triggered by the weight of the first truck. It worked exactly as Chris said it would. The explosions hurled chunks of concrete shrapnel at the convoy from both sides of the road, damaging or destroying every single vehicle.

As the dust and debris settled, a few of the trucks were still rolling, though not under their own power. They eventually thumped to a stop against trees or other trucks. An unnerving silence filled the air.

Now they waited. Chris said one of three things would likely happen in the next few minutes. The enemy would realize they were already beaten and would surrender, accepting their losses. Or they would begin firing wildly in a panic, thinking they were about to be slaughtered. They might also think this one big show was all Belle Plaine had to offer and they would quickly regroup and counterattack, thinking they could still salvage some kind of victory.

Whichever way it went, Chris said, no one was to open fire or show themselves unless the enemy fired first, or Chris or Ashley came out into the open to negotiate the enemy surrender.

A full minute passed. Finally, the door of one of the pickups creaked open and a man stumbled out. Dazed and still trying to get his bearings, he stood swaying back and forth before turning and going to the back of the truck. With great effort, he pulled himself into the bed of the pickup and took up position behind the fifty-caliber machine gun.

"Don't be stupid," Erik said in a low voice. He wished he had his rifle. He could take out the man with a single shot. But of all the men and women in the woods around him, he was the only one without a rifle or shotgun. He had only his pistol, his knife, and his staff. Eben and Chris had both suggested he not join in the actual fight but simply "costume up" as the bear. They said just knowing the bear was with them would give the villagers courage and moral support. Erik thought it sounded like a bunch of horseshit but he'd agreed to play along.

More men began climbing out of the trucks and the back of the second deuce-and-half. They were all armed and began taking up defensive positions. A stocky, older man with a long beard climbed up and manned a second fifty-caliber.

"I don't think they intend on surrendering," Erik whispered.

"If we stay down and don't give them anything to shoot at," Eben whispered back, "they may give up and go home to lick their wounds."

The stocky man with the beard let out a tribal scream and began firing, strafing the woods on Erik's side of the road, the machine gun making a rapid, thunderous *boom-boom-boom*. Slugs thudded into the trees, shredding limbs and branches. The man on the second machine gun also let out a holler and began strafing the trees on the other side. The men who had taken defensive positions in and around the trucks also began firing wildly into the woods.

"You were saying?" Erik hollered to Eben above the noise.

The villagers hidden on either side of the road began returning fire.

Erik's thoughts flashed back to the firefight at the mansion twenty years earlier. That battle was short and violent but it was over now.

The battle for Belle Plaine was just beginning.

***

Pierce fought his way back to consciousness and tried to focus on where he was. The truck was resting on its side. The cab was crushed down where it had slammed into the tree. There was broken glass, clods of dirt, grass, sticks, and leaves all over the inside of the cab. Orlando was still in his seat and behind the wheel above him, held in place by his seat belt. Blood was dripping from his head onto Pierce. Judging by the amount of blood he felt saturating his clothes, Pierce was pretty sure the man was dead.

What in the hell had happened? He remembered they had been approaching Belle Plaine. There were farmers working in the fields. He had been about to tell Orlando something. And then… Everything after that was a jumbled confusion of terrifying sights and sounds.

He slowly became aware of the sounds of gunfire. He could hear the thudding booms of the big machine guns and sharp cracks of automatic fire from M-16s. There was shouting. There were rapid pops of small-caliber rifle fire coming from all around.

The explosions. He remembered the road suddenly erupting all around them. Enormous slabs of pavement had been flying through the air. Smaller chunks, like a billion pieces of shrapnel, had peppered the truck and shattered the windshields. He felt the side of his face. It burned. His hand came away bloody.

The lead truck, the one with Burrows and Furman, had flipped backwards in the air towards them. Orlando had steered violently to avoid it.

Mines. Belle Plaine had mined the road. That was the only explanation. And now the continuous gunfire. Jesus Christ, the trees. They were stopped in a narrow gap between the trees and now his men were caught in the crossfire of God knew how many guns.

What in the hell went wrong? What had they gotten themselves into? They had been tricked. These weren't defenseless farmers at all. His men had been lured straight into an ambush and now they were being cut to pieces.

He had to do something. It couldn't end this way. He needed time to think.

He quickly felt his pants pockets, his jacket. There it was. Thank God it hadn't fallen out and been lost. He just hoped it still worked.

He pulled out one of only two working two-way radios he knew of still in existence. He pressed his thumb on the 'talk' button.

***

Images of the firefight in Elk River kept flashing through Ashley's mind. It was the only other time she'd ever been in the middle of anything like this. But this was much, much worse. The sound of those big machine guns in the backs of the trucks terrified her. They were tearing the hell out of the woods around them.

But as scared as she was, she was even more pissed off. These bastards thought they could roll in here and take everything her and her people had worked so hard to build over the years? No, that was not going to happen. Not today. Not ever.

She rose up from behind the logs she and Chris had taken cover behind, aimed, fired, and ducked back down. She doubted she was hitting anyone. She was usually a pretty fair shot but they were too far away and she was firing too quickly.

Next to her, Chris was in a one-knee stance, resting his rifle on one of the logs to steady his aim. He fired, paused, fired, paused, and fired again before ducking back down. Bullets slammed into the logs and the trees around them as someone on the road returned fire.

"I can't get a good shot at that machine gunner from here," Chris said. He glanced quickly to their right and then back to her. "If I can get to that tree over there, I'll have a better angle on him. Think you can cover me?"

Despite her fear and pumping adrenaline, she had to smile. "I'm your mother. You have to ask?" She turned and rested her rifle on the log, taking aim at a short, hairy little man ducking behind the back of a pickup. She paused, let her breath out slowly, and pulled the trigger. The man fell and rolled behind the rear tire, wounded but not dead. She turned to Chris.

"Go!"

As she was searching for another target, Chris sprinted across the short distance to the tree, keeping as low as he could. She saw the harry dwarf peek out from behind the tire and begin tracking Chris with his rifle. Ashley quickly sighted in on him again. "Eat shit, munchkin," she whispered and pulled the trigger. A mist of blood and gray matter exploded from the back of the dwarf's head.

Heavy slugs from one of the machine guns began slamming into the logs and tearing up the dirt like tiny explosions all around her position. She quickly dropped back down and lay as flat as she could, hugging the ground. She glanced up just long enough to confirm Chris had made it to the tree.

Chris was rising from a crouch. He steadied his rifle against the tree, aimed, and fired a single shot.

The continuous fire from the machine gun quickly tracked from Ashley's position to Chris's, taking out small trees and branches all along its path. Ashley caught her breath as she saw that Chris wasn't ducking back down. He was still holding his aim. As the air around Chris filled with splinters of wood and pieces of bark, he fired a second time.

The machine gun fell silent.

Chris looked over to her, grinned, and gave a thumbs-up.

She let out a shuddering breath and made a mental note to have a stern talk with her son about scaring the hell out of his mother once this was all over.

She sat back up and began searching for another target. The rifle fire to her right and from across the road had become more sporadic but she could still hear another big machine gun firing from up the road to her left. She glanced that way and saw a man crawling out of the broken windshield of one of the big trucks that was lying on its side against a tree. He was shorter than average and was wearing a blood-soaked, military dress uniform, complete with medals and ribbons. His face was streaked with blood.

Ashley sighted in on him and began tracking him as he scrambled up the side of the road. He was shouting something and waving his arms. She was about to pull the trigger when she realized he was shouting, "Cease fire! Cease fire!"

She kept her finger on the trigger but didn't pull it. The shooting from the road quickly petered out and then the rest of the sporadic fire ceased as well. The man was now standing in the middle of the road, still waving his arms.

Though she had never seen him before, she had no doubt who he was.

Pierce.

***

Eben stood and put his fingers to his mouth. He blew two long, shrill whistles. The shooting from the woods quickly died as the signal was repeated down the line from both sides of the road.

Erik also stood and watched the man in the road as he walked towards the trucks, still waving his arms but no longer shouting for a cease fire. He had to be the one who called himself Captain Pierce. Erik had never seen him before but wasn't surprised he was a short, squirrely looking man. If he remembered his history correctly, most dictators and fascists were.

What did surprise him was that Pierce was here at all. He couldn't imagine someone like Pierce putting himself in harm's way when he could just as easily send others to be killed in his place. But then Pierce had probably thought taking Belle Plaine was going to be a walk in the park. Not seeing any real danger to himself, he'd probably decided he wanted to "lead" his men to their biggest victory to date. Except, of course, they would do all the work while he took the credit for it.

What a dick, Erik thought.

Pierce's men were slowly climbing down and out from under and around the trucks. It looked like there were about ten or twelve of them still alive. Twenty or so were lying wounded or dead on the road. As the surviving men slowly formed up in a group in front of Pierce, Erik noted they weren't dropping their weapons.

"I wouldn't trust that asshole," he warned Eben, "not until all of his men are accounted for and every weapon is lying on the ground."

Pierce turned and surveyed the woods.

"I need someone I can talk to," he shouted.

"That would be you," Erik said. "If Pierce sees me right now, it'll probably send him into an apoplectic fit."

"No sweat," Eben said, placing his huge hand on Erik's shoulder. "We've got this covered. You just stay here and keep those sharp eyes of yours on things. If you see anyone trying to outflank or blindside us, give a shout."

"Can't I just shoot them?" Erik asked, indicating the pistol in his belt. "Please?"

"Use your best judgment. But starting the shooting again right now may not be in everybody's best interest." He nodded toward the road. "Especially not theirs."

Erik followed his nod and saw Ashley and Chris emerging from the woods on the other side of the road.

***

Pierce turned at the sound of someone coming up onto the road behind him and laid eyes on the most striking woman he'd ever seen. She was tall and carried herself with a poise and confidence he'd never seen in even his most trusted men. She had beautiful green eyes and dark brown, almost black hair that fell past her shoulders. With her was a tall young man who couldn't be much over twenty years old, if even that. He had lighter hair but shared her green eyes.

Mother and son?

As they approached, the sound of a third person coming onto the road caused him to turn again. He felt his heart suddenly speed up. Was this the bear? The man was well-over six feet tall, with broad shoulders and blonde hair. He looked exceedingly strong. The only thing that didn't fit was the man was not wearing a bear-skin coat or carrying the big staff of hickory rumored to be the bear's most-feared weapon.

The man joined the woman and boy on the road in front of him. They positioned themselves so Pierce was between them and his men – clever. If anyone of his men fired at them, they risked hitting him as well. They were each carrying a rifle and each was pointed in his general direction.

He had to stall for time. He had no idea how many of these so-called farmers were in the woods on either side of the road, these "farmers" who had just decimated his heavily armed and experienced militia.

"I am Colonel Pierce," he started. "I need to know who I can talk to before this goes any farther."

"*Colonel?*" the woman said, her voice dripping with disdain. "That's quite a jump in rank from captain, though you were never really a captain either. Were you?"

"There doesn't need to be any more fighting," Pierce said, ignoring her disrespectful tone. "I'm sure we can come to a reasonable arrangement."

"Like the 'arrangement' you made with St. Peter?" the boy asked. "Or Waseca, or Faribault, or Owatonna?"

"We're well aware of how your arrangements work, *Colonel*," the woman said. "A lot of the people in Belle Plaine have come from towns you've pillaged and plundered. They don't have good things to say about you or your men. As you might have guessed by now, a lot of them are in these trees right now with their rifles aimed directly at you. It's only a single word from any of us here that's stopping them from blowing you away right now."

"You have nothing we could possibly want or need," the blonde giant said. "You should have heeded our warning and turned back when you could."

"So, what now?" Pierce asked. "You just gun me and my men down in the street? You slaughter us like cows?"

"You and your men are free to go," the woman said. "We're decent people, unlike yourself. You lay your weapons at your feet, you turn around and leave, and you never return. That's the only arrangement you're going to get today."

In the distance, Pierce heard the sound he'd been waiting for. It was coming up fast. He turned to address the people hidden in the woods, hoping to distract these assholes and buy himself another minute or two.

"People of Belle Plaine," he called, raising his voice, "listen to me. It doesn't have to be this way. We have working vehicles, fuel, electricity – enough for everyone. You don't have to endure another cold winter. You have crops and livestock. You know the land and how to make it produce. We respect that. But please let us help you. Let our machines do the labor for you. We can both benefit. Together, we can build something bigger and greater than either of us has alone. Let's *all* lay down our weapons. Together we can rebuild civilization and make a better world for everyone."

His timing was perfect. At that moment, the first Humvee came roaring up the side of the road, swerving to avoid the wrecked trucks and hunks of pavement but not quite all the dead bodies. Vlad was standing in the back, both hands on the fifty-caliber, somehow maintaining his balance as the vehicle swerved and bounced and jumped.

The armored, incredibly agile vehicle ramped up the ditch and landed on the road between him and his men. The driver steered the Humvee in an expert drift and skidded to a halt not three feet from him. Jules was in the passenger seat, looking as calm and collected as always.

Vlad immediately swung the machine gun on the three people standing apart from Pierce. He pulled the bolt back, locking and loading.

The second Humvee, also with a mounted machine gun, roared up the other side of the road and screeched to a halt next to the first. The gunner on this one also swung his weapon on the men and woman on the road and also locked and loaded.

Pierce's men stepped back, closer to the cover of the trucks, raising their weapons and pointing them to the trees on either side of the road.

Pierce smiled and nodded. Orlando had been right to suggest holding some of his forces back, but Pierce had only partly taken his advice. He'd had the Humvees trail the convoy and then stop and wait just a couple of miles down the road, ready to charge in if and when they were needed.

This was priceless. He turned to the blonde man, the woman, and the kid, expecting to see fear, shock, resignation on their faces. Instead, he saw... nothing. They looked as if they didn't even see the fifty-calibers pointed at them. Either that, or they didn't care.

"Now we renegotiate," Pierce growled stepping up to the woman. Though it baffled him, he was sure now she was the one in charge. "One word from me and Vlad will turn you, your kid, and this big motherfucker here into hamburger. I don't care how many people you have in those woods. You three will die and then so will all of them. And then we'll burn your precious little town to the ground and piss on the ashes. Do you understand me?"

The blonde man raised his fingers to his lips and gave a single, sharp whistle. From the woods all around came the ratcheting of rifle bolts being drawn back and shotguns being pumped. Pierce couldn't count them all but it sounded like a lot. Someone lobbed a heavy, brown, egg-shaped object from out of the trees. It bounced and rolled to a stop at Pierce's feet.

It was a hand grenade. The pin was still in it.

What the fuck?

The woman took a step forward. She spoke in a low, steely voice, her green eyes as cold as winter ice.

"Now you listen to me, you dickless wonder. Do you think this little fireworks show that just destroyed all of your trucks was all we had? You've got to be some kind of moron. My offer still stands. You turn around and leave right now and you live. It doesn't matter if you kill me or anyone else standing here. The moment you do, the men and women in those trees will open fire with everything they have, and they absolutely will not stop until every goddamned one of you is dead. And then they will go back to their homes. They will eat their suppers and they will forget all about you. This is *their* town, not mine. This is what you're up against. This is what you cannot defeat."

Pierce felt his heart racing. The blood was pounding in his head. This fucking bitch. Who the hell did she think she was talking to? Fuck her. Fuck all of them. If they wanted to die for a bunch of cows and a few stocks of corn, he'd goddamn well oblige them. He began to raise his hand to signal Vlad when he caught sight of someone stepping out of the woods behind the three in front of him. He was a big man. He was wearing a heavy fur coat and carrying a thick, wooden staff.

Finally. The bear!

***

Erik stepped onto the road and approached the show-down that was taking place. He knew Ashley would not back down. This town and its people were too important to her. And everything he knew or had heard about Pierce told him that, even in the face of assured destruction, his ego would never let him admit defeat. If he was going down, he would take everyone with him. Unless Erik did something drastic and did it quick, this was going to end only one way – in a bloodbath.

He noted how Pierce's men began shuffling slightly and whispering back and forth as soon as he stepped onto the road. Maybe there was something to what Eben and Chris had said after all, about him "costuming up," though just not in the way they thought.

"What in the hell are you doing?" Ashley hissed at him.

"Probably something stupid," he whispered back. He positioned himself between Pierce and Ashley and stood with his staff planted firmly in front of himself.

Pierce, his face all cut up and bloody, scowled at him. Beyond Pierce, Erik saw the Viking that had been about to behead Dean in Jordan standing in the back of the Humvee with his hands on the machine gun. In the driver's seat of the Humvee was a man Erik didn't recognize.

The passenger side door opened and the big black man from under the trees in Mankato stepped out. The man closed the door and then stood there, looking in his direction with a completely neutral expression on his face. Erik noted he was the only person in Pierce's militia who was not carrying a gun or weapon of any kind. He again wondered who he was and what part he was playing in all of this.

"So, the bear finally shows himself," Pierce sneered. "Did you really think you could scare me away with your little stunt in Jordan, or with your pathetic threat after ambushing my men on the road?"

When Erik didn't reply, he continued. "I know Corporal McClain sent you up here. I hear you and him were real good buddies a long time ago. Did you think it would do any good?" He waited for a reaction. When none came, he added, "He's dead, you know, executed as a traitor. Parsons and all the other rats too."

Erik felt a sudden flash of anger but kept it in check, keeping his expression impassive. The bastard had killed McClain and everyone who had been working with him, all because McClain had tried to save a few lives.

"Did you really think you could protect these people?" Pierce asked. "Why don't you just crawl back into your cave or wherever the hell you came from before you get anyone else killed?"

Erik tilted his head slightly and glanced past Pierce to his men. His gaze moved from one man to the next. In every face, he saw a man who didn't want to be here. In every face, he saw a man who would rather be back at home with his wife or his friends. None of them wanted to die today.

His gaze shifted back to Pierce.

"I told you I would kill you if you came to Belle Plaine. Your men can leave. You will not."

Pierce hesitated, then grinned and said, "So it's me you want. You kill me and that solves everyone's problems, is that it? A little one on one? *Mano a mano*? Winner takes all?" He leaned forward and whispered, "Do you think I'm stupid?"

Stepping back, he turned to his men and raised his voice.

"We have a problem here, men. It seems that *the bear* has promised to kill me. But I have also made a promise. I promised his head to Vlad." He raised his arm and motioned for the Viking to step down from the Humvee. He then pointed to the driver to take the Viking's place at the machine gun.

The Viking jumped from the Humvee and walked over to stand next to Pierce.

"My proposal is this." Pierce turned and pointed to Erik. "The bear..." He pointed with his other arm to the Viking. "Versus Vlad."

"I don't speak for the town or these people," Erik said.

"We're not playing for the town anymore, you idiot. You said you were going to kill me. Well, now's your chance. But you have to go through my man first. You beat him and no one's going to stop you. If he takes your head, I take my men and we leave, but he keeps your head as a trophy. Either way, this shithole town is safe, at least for a while. Do we have a deal?"

"Erik, no," Ashley said from behind him. "He's beaten already. You don't have to do anything more."

"She's right," Pierce said, "you don't have to do anything. Me and my men could leave right now, but we'll be back. And don't think we'll make the same mistakes twice. The next time we come, we *will* take this town. Or your people can try to gun us down where we stand. You might kill all of us but not before you take a lot more casualties."

He turned and motioned to the machine gunner standing in the back of the second Humvee. The man bent down and reached for something. When he stood up again, he was holding a long metal tube on his shoulder with a projectile at the end.

"That's an RPG, a rocket-propelled grenade. We've got quite a few of these. We start shooting them into the trees, how many of your people do you think are going to go home tonight to eat their suppers?" He paused for effect, his gaze shifting between Erik and Ashley.

"It's your choice."

Erik looked at Ashley. He'd never seen fear in her eyes before, not even when the cult attacked the mansion, but he saw it now. She shook her head slightly and mouthed the word *No*.

Eben and Chris also looked worried but he could tell they understood what was at stake here. If he declined to fight and let Pierce and his men leave, Belle Plaine would always live under the threat of imminent attack, and another attack would eventually come. When it did, Pierce would not underestimate this bunch of farmers again. The next time, Belle Plaine would fall. Their only choice was to accept Pierce's challenge – kill his man and then kill Pierce himself.

He looked back to Ashley and gave her a slight shrug and a smile.

"What can I do? I'm supposed to be the hero, right?"

He took off his coat and gun belt, handing both to Eben.

***

As Pierce stepped back, Vlad pulled the battle ax from his belt and took a wide stance. Holding the weapon in one hand, he grinned and hunched forward towards Erik. He uttered a low, menacing growl and began circling to his right.

Erik held his staff in both hands and quickly checked behind himself to make sure Ashley, Eben, and Chris were clear. The instant his eyes shifted, Vlad lunged forward and swung his ax, missing Erik's chest by less than an inch.

He jumped back and to the side. Before Vlad could recover from his swing, he stepped forward again and caught the Viking across the back of the shoulders with his staff. There was an audible, heavy thump but Vlad quickly moved out of range, not even shrugging off the blow. Had he even felt it?

Vlad grinned even more fiercely, recovering from his swing and continuing to circle slowly. Erik held his ground and pivoted to follow him. Vlad was staying just out of range of his staff. As they circled each other, Erik was dimly aware of Pierce's men edging closer to get a better view of the match.

This is going to end quickly, he thought, acknowledging the big man's skill. *The first person to make a mistake is going to die.*

Vlad suddenly lunged forward a step and then just as quickly stepped back. Erik didn't fall for the feint. He kept pivoting, holding his staff in the middle, ready to swing either end or to suddenly jab it forward. A scene from an old movie flashed through his mind and he wished he hadn't handed his pistol and holster to Eben. He could have just stepped back, drew his revolver, and shot this ugly bastard.

Vlad feinted again. This time Erik did a quick side-step and hit Vlad with a rapid one-two-three to the knees, ribs, and head before the man could step back. The headshot caused Vlad to stagger but he quickly shook it off. He let out a roar and charged straight at Erik, holding his ax at shoulder height.

Erik spun backwards and swung his staff around to connect with the back of Vlad's knees, hoping to take his legs out from under him or at least trip him up. But Vlad suddenly stopped, reversed, and spun backwards too, bringing his ax back around in a wide, flat arc.

Erik had a moment's thought, *Damn, that's a good move*, as he felt the razor-sharp blade slice across the front of his neck.

He heard gasps and hisses from the crowd.

"Erik!" Ashley cried.

It stung like hell but he managed to keep his focus and take a couple of quick steps back, bringing his staff back up to its ready position. Vlad was circling again, a combined grin and snarl on his face. Erik could feel blood running down his neck and chest but there was no blood on the edge of Vlad's ax. Jesus, had he really swung it so fast the blood hadn't touched it? Or was the edge so sharp blood couldn't stick to it?

As Erik pivoted to keep his opponent in front of him, he became aware of his own raspy breathing. He tasted blood in his mouth. Shit. That cut was a lot deeper than he'd thought. Blood was running into his throat and lungs. He fought the urge to cough. He needed to finish this before he choked to death on his own blood.

The sight of Erik's blood excited Vlad. He sensed imminent victory now. His grin grew broader, exposing even more teeth, and he shifted his ax quickly from one hand to the other and then back again. He was itching to come in for the kill.

"I don't think he really killed a bear," he heard one of Pierce's men say. "Not with that stupid stick anyway."

An image of the grizzly bear as it had reared up on its hind legs before swiping at him with its claws flashed through Erik's head. He stumbled and dropped to one knee, coughing and spraying blood across the broken pavement. He heard Ashley shouting something but she sounded so far away. Staring at his own blood on the road in front of himself, he heard his staff clatter to the pavement and roll away from him.

Vlad let out a tremendous, victorious roar and moved in for the kill, bringing his ax around in a high arc over his shoulder.

Mistake, Erik thought.

Just as Vlad was bringing his ax down with everything he had, Erik pulled the Bowie knife from his belt and launched himself forwards, catching Vlad across the midsection with his shoulder as Chris had done to him in the saloon. With every last bit of strength he had, he drove Vlad backwards against the front of the Humvee, slamming him against the grill. He quickly brought the Bowie knife up and rammed it into the side of the Viking wannabe's neck.

Erik held him there, his hand still on the handle of the knife. It had gone to the hilt. The end of the blade was protruding from the other side of the man's neck. A massive amount of blood was spurting from both wounds.

Vlad's eyes were wide and his mouth open, cut off mid-roar. As Erik watched, the life faded from Vlad's eyes and his face went slack. The great spurts of blood abruptly stopped. He heard Vlad's ax drop to the pavement.

He jerked his knife out of the man's neck and stepped back. The lifeless body continued standing for a second or two, held up by the front of the Humvee. Then it slid down the vehicle's grill and slumped to the ground.

He turned and saw Pierce standing just a few feet away. He was staring at Vlad, his expression a mix of disbelief and rage. Erik tried to say something but all that came out was a choking sound and a spray of blood from the front of his throat. He felt himself swaying, his strength rapidly draining away. He dropped to one knee and then the other. His vision was growing darker around the edges.

Pierce's enraged gaze swung briefly to Erik and then up to the machine gunner on the Humvee.

"Kill them," Pierce shouted, swinging his arm. "Kill them all!"

"Hold!" a second voice bellowed. "Stand down!" It was loud, deep, and reverberated from everywhere.

He turned his head. Though his vision was quickly dimming, he could see the large black man from under the trees at Mankato. The man had one hand raised to Pierce's men.

"Colonel Pierce has gone back on his word," the man said. His deep, bass voice carried strength and authority. "He has led us into an ambush and he has no honor. He is no longer fit to lead. I am assuming command. Lay down your weapons. It is done. This is over."

There was a general murmuring from the men on the road and then the clatter of weapons being dropped to the ground.

"What the fuck do you think you're doing?" Pierce screamed at the man. "This is *my* army. These are *my* men." He struggled to undo the flap of the holster at his side and draw his pistol.

From the corner of his eye, Erik saw Ashley striding up behind Pierce. She was holding his revolver in her hand. He saw her cock the pistol, raise it, and fire at point-blank range in a single, fluid move.

One half of Pierce's head exploded in a spray of blood, brains, and bone. His knees buckled and his body crumpled to the ground like a marionette with its strings suddenly cut.

Erik tried to hold on to his fading consciousness. He was sure Ashley would say something like, "You're relieved of command, motherfucker" and he wanted to hear it.

But then he felt himself slumping to his side and everything went black.

JUNE 1

A low mist swirled around his feet, revealing brief glimpses of the forest floor beneath as he walked. It was one of those surreal mornings where the woods were so quiet and still, he could have believed he was the only living thing moving among the trees.

As he walked, he held his hands out to his sides and let the damp leaves and grass slide across his fingers. He reached out and held onto a small walnut tree as he stepped over a moss-slick log, feeling the rough bark against the palm of his hand. Somewhere up ahead and to his left, he could hear water trickling over the rocks in a creek bed.

This was his home. A long time ago, a time he could barely remember now, he had lived somewhere else. There had been a house. There had been people smiling and talking and laughing. There had been meals around a table and a warm, comfortable bed every night.

The memories were tenuous, fleeting and shifting, like the mist at his feet. If he tried hard enough, sometimes he could remember little things like a young girl with blonde hair and blue eyes, or a white cat with black on its tail and between its ears, with just a smidgeon of brown mixed in. But as the days passed into years, those memories had become more distant, harder to recall and hold onto.

A flash of bright color up ahead, out of place among the greens and browns of the forest. Curious, he pushed ahead through knee-high grass and sycamores, coming to a small clearing where the mist was thicker and lay like a mysterious white cloud, hiding the ground beneath. A small, leafless tree rose up from the mist in the center of the clearing, its long, thin branches reaching up and out like skeletal fingers. A bright silver chain was looped over one of the branches. Turning slowly at the end of the chain, just above the mist, was a small, dark blue rabbit.

He reached out and took the chain from the branch. He held it up and studied the rabbit curiously as it turned in a slow circle. It was solid and heavy for its size. It was shaped from some kind of deep-blue stone and polished smooth until it reflected even the softest light.

Magic bunny.

Where had that come from? It seemed to mean something, something he could almost grasp.

Sam...

Thoughts, memories of a young girl with long, blonde hair and blue eyes began flooding in. Still staring at the necklace, trying to focus on the memories crowding his mind, he turned to leave the clearing. He took a couple of steps and glanced up. An old woman with long, graying hair was standing in front of him, a kindly smile on her age-lined face. Her hands were folded in front of her. She was dressed in deerskins with a blanket over her shoulders. She seemed familiar but he couldn't remember ever seeing her before.

"You have done well, Erik," the old woman said. "You should rest now, for a little while."

"No," he heard himself saying. "I have to find Sam. I promised I would come back for her."

The old woman nodded once and continued smiling, a patient, understanding look in her eyes.

"She knows, Erik. You kept your promise and she knows that. But she wants you to rest now. In time, she will find you."

The soft, white mist of the forest turned gray and thick, rising up all around to engulf him. The old woman faded away. The clearing was gone. The forest was gone. There was only the darkening, gray fog. It pressed against him from all sides, like some cruel, insidious thing, alive and determined not to let him go.

He struggled against it, fighting nausea and vertigo. It was like swimming through tar. But with one last surge of effort, he broke through, free of the growing darkness.

He opened his eyes and gasped for breath.

He was in a bed back at the farmhouse in Belle Plaine. The lights were off but there was an oil lantern burning on the table next to the bed. The flame was low, barely illuminating the room.

Turning his head, he felt something pull at his neck. Chris was there, sitting in a chair next to the bed, a book in his hands. Behind him, the windows were dark. He must have been out for hours.

Chris was staring at him, a look of surprise on his face.

"Holy shit!" he exclaimed. "You're awake! You're *alive!*" He dropped the book on the table and got to his feet. "Don't move. Don't try to talk. I'll go get Mom."

Erik opened his mouth to say something but Chris was already sprinting from the room. He reached up and touched the thick bandages on his throat. God, he was weak. He felt tired and completely drained of energy. How much blood had he lost?

His mouth was dry as sand. He turned his head one way and then the other, looking for a glass of water, a beer... anything wet.

Ashley came rushing into the room with Chris right behind. She stopped, staring at him, and then burst into tears and rushed to the bed. She knelt and took his hand, squeezing hard.

"Oh my god." She was crying and laughing at the same time. "You're awake. You had me so scared but you're awake now. You're alive. Oh my god."

"Calm down, Mom," Chris said, grinning and having regained his own composure. "Geeze. He is the bear after all. You didn't think something as wimpy as a battle ax could kill him, did you?"

Erik reached over with his other hand and placed it on top of Ashley's. She leaned forward and kissed his hand and then pressed her cheek against it, still crying.

Eben came in and crossed the room to the other side of the bed. He was holding a glass of water with a straw in it.

"Only a sip or two at first," he said, lowering the glass and placing the straw between Erik's lips. "You can have some more in a bit. You drink too much too fast and you'll throw up and probably tear all those stitches loose."

Erik sucked on the straw and felt the cool water wash across his tongue and down his throat. He didn't think anything ever tasted so welcome and refreshing in all his life. He took another sip and then Eben pulled the straw back.

"That's enough for now." Eben set the glass on the table. "I'll leave it here. You can have some more in a bit once we're sure you can keep it down."

"What...," Erik started to say and felt a burning sting in his throat. The word didn't come out at all, just a hiss of air. He swallowed and was going to try again when Eben stopped him.

"Don't try to talk. You took some damage to your larynx from that ax. Would have been a lot worse if that big guy didn't keep the blade razor-sharp, but it's still going to be awhile. Don't rush it."

He glanced down at Ashley. Her head was up and she was smiling at him, her cheeks still wet with tears. He tried to say her name but nothing came out. She looked like she was going to start crying again.

A wave a fatigue washed over him and he felt his eyes closing. Just before he drifted off, he heard Eben talking again. His words seemed to come from the end of a long tunnel.

"Don't worry, he's just sleeping. He's going to be in and out for a while until his strength returns."

JUNE 4

When he opened his eyes again, sunlight was streaming in through the open window. A cool breeze was billowing the curtains. The air smelled like spring.

Eben was dozing in the chair next to the bed. They were apparently taking shifts. He glanced around and spied the glass of water with the straw. It took all his strength to sit up and snag the glass off the table. Nearly exhausted from the effort, he sat back against the headboard, resting and catching his breath.

"I could have gotten that for you," Eben said, his eyes open now.

"I'm fine." His voice was little more than a whisper. It had a raspy, sandpapery sound to it. He felt a kind of pinching deep in his throat. He took a few sips of water.

"You're not fine but you're getting there," Eben said. "You must have the constitution of an ox. If you're up for it, I'll bring you some warm soup."

Erik took another sip of water and again noted the open window and the light breeze blowing in. The smell of the breeze, added to how weak and tired he felt, implied this was *not* the morning after.

"How long was I out?" The water eased the pinched feeling in his throat but failed to improve the quality of his voice.

"You were in a coma for four days. You lost a lot of blood. I can't even imagine how you survived. And you've been in and out for another two days, so it's been about a week. You probably don't remember much."

"Not much," Erik agreed. He reached up and touched the bandages on his throat. "Who's the doctor?"

Eben smiled. "Ashley, with my assistance of course. Unfortunately, we don't have a proper surgeon in town but it looks like she learned just enough from Saundra to save your life. Believe me when I say, she's the only one who really believed you would pull through. She never gave up hope."

"Where is she?"

"She'll be back in a couple of hours. She's out meeting with Jules, hammering out trade arrangements and how this new-found peace accord is going to work."

"Jules?"

"That big man who was with Pierce. The one that called a halt to the fighting and relieved Pierce of his command just before Ashley blew his brains out. The one who picked you up off that road and carried you here. He's in charge of Mankato now and he's already making some major changes. Pretty good for a blind man."

Erik was surprised. "Blind? No shit?"

"Said he's been blind since birth. Not many people ever figure it out right away. He's so attuned to his other senses most people just assume he can see as well as they can. I didn't even realize it myself until he'd brought you all the way up here and I asked him to hand me a pair of scissors from the table."

Standing, he said, "I'll go make you that soup now. Beef and vegetable. Maybe I'll even throw in a slice of bread. You haven't eaten anything but watery broth for the last six days and you probably don't even remember that."

"Could explain why I'm so hungry."

Eben gave a final nod and walked out of the room. Moments later, Chris peered around the edge of the doorway.

"You awake?"

Erik nodded.

Chris came in and pulled the chair a little closer to the bed before sitting in it.

"Don't worry, I'm not going to stay long. We're still cleaning up that mess out on the road and trying to get it into decent shape for the trucks."

"Trucks?"

"From Mankato. They're bringing us up a couple of big generators and some more fuel. They're even going to leave one of the trucks here for us to use. Didn't Eben tell you? Mom and Jules, that big guy, are working overtime on this new partnership."

"He mentioned it."

"That Jules is a pretty amazing guy. I don't know why he didn't take Pierce out earlier and take control himself, but I guess he had his reasons. Did you know he's blind?"

"Eben told me."

Chris nodded and looked down at the floor. When he looked up again, he said, "What you did back there on the road... When you took on that big Viking bastard... That was pretty amazing. Real hero-type stuff."

"I don't think your mother would agree."

"I always wondered about you. She said you were only fifteen when she met you but she's always talked like you were this unsung hero of the apocalypse, about how you had more bravery, character, and honor than anyone she'd ever met. I guess I never really understood what she meant until you stepped up onto that road and put yourself between us and that big Viking, that army. You were willing to die to protect everyone."

"I stole your move," Erik said, trying to deflect the praise, "the one you used against me in the bar."

Chris chuckled. "I saw that. But kneeling, dropping your staff and faking him out like that... That was brilliant..., and pretty goddamn risky."

"I was only half faking. I didn't think I would last much longer. But then one of his men said something about me killing that bear and I knew I could take him out the same way, if I could just get him close enough."

"Like I said, pretty goddamn risky. If your foot had slipped, or if he had turned..." Chris shook his head. "Most everyone in town saw what you did. And if they didn't see it, they've heard about it by now, even down in Mankato. You were a myth for many before, a rumor people passed around. Now you're a bona fide goddamn legend."

Erik didn't say anything. He had always been uncomfortable being the object of attention. He tolerated Ashley's "hero" talk just because..., well, just because she was Ashley. But if he was becoming the object of some sort of hero worship, he may just have to disappear back into the woods for a few more years.

"You know what people in town are calling me now?" Chris asked.

Erik shook his head.

"Bear cub." He laughed. "I don't think I like that, not the 'cub' part anyway. Makes me sound like a little kid."

"SOB," Erik suggested. "Son of Bear."

Chris laughed again. "There! That sounds better. I could live with that." He turned his head and stared out the window a moment. When he looked back to Erik, he said, "But better still, I think, is your son. That's who I really am."

Chris reached over and took Erik's hand in both of his and squeezed.

"I'm glad to have you as a father, and I would be damn proud to call you Dad."

***

"So, we've made arrangements for two generators, fuel, and a truck," Ashley was saying, lying beside him on the bed. "And we're sending down half a dozen people to help them get set up in farming and to help build a couple of greenhouses."

She was trailing her fingertips lightly up and down his chest, making it difficult for him to concentrate on what she was saying.

"We've got enough in reserve to help them through this next winter," she continued. "After that, they should be able to sustain themselves. And Eben has started working with them on plans to begin moving south. Not right away. This is going to take a lot of planning and co-ordination, but within two, three years he hopes."

She paused and glanced up at him. "Are you hearing anything I'm saying?"

He grinned. "What you're doing with your hand, it's a little distracting." His voice was still no more than a rasping whisper.

"Really?" She moved her hand to his stomach. "How about now?"

"Getting *really* distracting." He pulled her closer.

"Oh no you don't, mister," she said, moving her hand back to his chest. "That's as far as I go. Give those stitches at least another week to heal. *Then* maybe we can talk about going a little lower."

He sighed. "A week is too long. Five days?"

"Let me see." She carefully peeled the edge of the bandage back and studied his neck. "Damn, I think Eben is right. You *do* have the constitution of an ox." She replaced the bandage. "Four days, but only if you're back to your normal appetite."

"Start roasting the pig."

She laid her head on his chest.

"I don't think your voice is going to get much better. That ax cut right through your larynx. Your vocal cords were nearly severed."

"Small price to pay," he said, and then remembered what he was thinking of just before he lost consciousness.

"Did you say anything to Pierce as you blew his head off?"

She raised her head and frowned at him. "What?"

"When you shot Pierce in the head. I passed out right then. I've always wondered, did you make some cool, smart-ass comment?"

"Like what?"

"Like, 'You're relieved of command, motherfucker,' or something like that."

She stared at him a moment longer and then she smiled, shaking her head.

"That's what *you* would do. You're the king of smart-ass comments. I think you got it from Tyler. I swear to God, your last words in this life will be, 'Fuck you,' even if it takes your last breath."

"That's good. I'll have to remember that. But did you?"

"Sorry to disappoint you, but no. I just shot him and that was that. I didn't think he deserved any kind of eulogy, smart-assed or not. Next time, tell me you want me to say something witty and clever before you pull a stunt like that and I have to execute some tin-pot dictator."

He pulled her closer.

"I'm not sorry for what I did. I thought it was the only way to protect everyone. I'd do it again if I had to."

"I know you would. You did what you had to do, like always. And Jules agrees with you. He said if you hadn't stepped up like that and accepted Pierce's challenge, there would have been a lot more deaths that night. He knew Pierce better than anyone, and he said there was no way Pierce was going to leave without either your head or the heads of a lot of innocent people."

"What an asshole. I'm glad you killed him."

"I'm glad he's dead. Apparently, a lot of other people are glad too. I hear I'm almost as big a hero as you are now."

Erik hugged her again.

"Welcome to the hero club. It sucks but... well, it sucks."

She snuggled against him. He felt himself dozing off again when Ashley suddenly sat up and reached into her shirt pocket.

"I almost forgot..." She pulled out the silver chain with the blue amethyst rabbit – Sam's magic bunny. "I told you we had a good metal worker here. He fixed this for you. He can't guarantee it's bear-proof but he says it ought to last a good long while." She placed it in his hand.

Erik held up the chain and watched the rabbit twirl in the light. He thought of Sam and of the dream he'd had while he'd been in a coma. He tried to remember what the old woman said to him but it was just out of reach.

"I know Eben and Chris have already asked you this," Ashley said, "but I have to know." She had an expectant, anxious look in her eyes. "When you get better, when you're all healed up and you have your strength back, are you going to stay here with us, with me, or are you going to go back to your woods?" She paused and then quickly added, "Not that I'm pressuring you or anything. I'll accept whatever you want to do. You don't owe me anything and I don't have any claim over you."

Watching the little stone rabbit twirl in the light, he asked, "Remember that story I told you about the hidden lake I found in the woods, with the waterfall and the cottonwood trees?"

She nodded.

"I've been back up that way a lot of times over the years, but I've never been able to find that lake again. What I learned from that is, when you find something beautiful and rare, you hold onto it for as long as you can, because you may never find it again."

He slipped the necklace over her head, laying the pendant against her neck.

"I walked away from you once twenty years ago. If you want me to stay, if you'll have me, I'll never walk away again."

She kissed him softly on the lips and laid her head on his chest.

"I do."